the beef princess of practical county

the
beef
princess
of
practical
county

michelle houts

SCHOLASTIC INC.
New York Toronto London Auckland
Sydney Mexico City New Delhi Hong Kong

ISBN 978-0-545-29245-0

12 11 10 9 8 7 6 5 4 3 2 1   10 11 12 13 14 15/0

Printed in the U.S.A.   40

First Scholastic printing, September 2010

The text of this book is set in Goudy.
Book design by Kenny Holcomb

For Olivia, Seth, and Maggie.
You're all champions in my book.

the
beef
princess
of
practical
county

PROLOGUE

The arena glowed in the summer night. The stands filled quickly with a chattery buzz as spectators carrying elephant ears and lemon shake-ups took their seats. From inside the barn, I caught a glimpse of Carol Ann in the bleachers with her parents. Ronnie was out there too, with Frannie. And Mom and Granddad. Dad stood at the end of the arena.

I couldn't think about anything. I had to keep my mind clear. No, not clear, blank. *Block it all out,* I told myself. I didn't hear the rustle of the impatient animals around me. I didn't hear the distant screams of the terrified, thrilled passengers on the Super Loop. And I tried my best not to hear the auctioneer's voice from out in the ring as he began his seller's song.

Beside me, my steer huffed as if trying to pull my thoughts back into the barn, away from the state of blankness I tried desperately to maintain.

Don't look, whatever you do, don't look.

If I looked I might see those beautiful eyes, framed so perfectly by those long, wispy lashes. It was bad enough that I could feel him tugging slightly at the lead rope, his every movement pulling me closer to his living, breathing side.

I ran my hand along his back and patted his smooth, sleek shoulder without looking at him. I mumbled to him to be patient. Stupid old steer anyway. His impatience only proved his ignorance. He didn't even know enough about what was going on *not* to want to go out into the ring.

Of course, how could he know? After all, Dad and I had bathed him and groomed him just the same as we had done for every show this past week. And here he stood in a fancy halter, thinking he was headed out for competition one more time. How could a twelve-hundred-pound steer possibly comprehend what would happen next?

Merely thinking about it brought the burn of tears back into my eyes. Hadn't there been enough tears in the past few days? *Get it together, Lib. You're not going out there bawling like a baby.*

Suddenly the line moved forward. The hindquarters of the stocky Shorthorn steer in front of us took a step and so did we. One step closer to the inevitable.

Don't listen. Don't look. Don't think. Just go. Just go.

The tears were actually easier to hold back than the awful urge to stop moving. I wanted to freeze time at this very second so I could throw my arms around him and squeeze.

So I could bury my face in his warm, soft neck and smell the sweet mixture of straw and shampoo. So I could tell him I loved him and I was so proud of him.

So I could say "Goodbye" and "I'm sorry."

The Shorthorn took another step and suddenly we were out of the barn and into the glaring lights of the arena. The urge to freeze was climbing to a higher place inside me.

Just go. Just go.

ONE

— granddad's pasture —

They were total opposites from the very beginning. It was almost a year ago that I first saw them. It was a sunny Saturday morning in early September, and if I hadn't seen a calendar, I would have thought it was still midsummer. The air was heavy and sticky already at nine-thirty in the morning, when Dad, Frannie, and I piled out of the rusty old pickup at the gate to Granddad's pasture.

I loved the pasture. It always gave me a comfortable, kind of homey feeling. There was just something about acres and acres of green with big brown and black dots scattered all over, slowly moving and munching, like furry lawn mowers, keeping the grass all even and neatly trimmed. But pasture ground was a rare sight in Practical County.

"Northern Indiana farm ground's just too good for pasturing," I'd heard Dad say many times. What he meant was a man could earn a better profit raising a crop of corn or soybeans than he could growing grass for cattle to eat.

That was why Granddad's pasture was so perfect. With little rolling hills, a winding creek that cut a jagged path diagonally through it, and a couple of acres of woods, it would have been a nightmare to till, plant, and harvest.

As we stood at the gate, all of Granddad's calves loped eagerly over to greet us. All but one. In fact, that one acted downright uninterested in any of us while his herdmates licked our hands with their long, rough tongues.

The week-old calves wrapped their tongues around my fingers and tugged. That's a calf's way of saying, "Pleased to make your acquaintance," Dad had explained when I was no bigger than Frannie, my four-year-old sister, who at that moment was walking the fence. I watched her teetering, arms out straight, her mess of blond curls flapping behind as she placed one tennis-shoed foot after the other on the top rail. Where she had gotten those blond curls was a mystery. My own stick-straight, mousy brown hair came from the Ryan side. I ponytailed it daily, because there wasn't much else I could do with it.

While Frannie planted herself firmly on a fence post, I stared out across acres and acres of grass still green from summer but chewed to the very roots by the hungry herd inside the fence. The new calves at the gate were checking us out with the same curiosity we were showing to them. I set my mind on finding the calves with the most potential for steer stardom. I was looking for a steer calf that would take the Practical County Fair by storm.

The Practical County Fair. It was nothing short of the best week of the year in Practical County. Everyone in the community pretty much stopped whatever they were doing to come to the fair. It was where for one week you could do what you couldn't the whole rest of the year. Like eat elephant ears. Or sit inside the Grange tent sipping milk shakes and catching up with the neighbors. For some folks, the fair was a chance to show off their finest whatever. To pick that perfect rose and display it in a vase to see if it could earn the blue ribbon. Or wow the judges with a deep-dish apple crumb pie from Great-grandma's secret recipe. For a handful of others, it wasn't about competing but about coming to see it all. The exhibits, the animal shows, the annual Beef Princess pageant, and the neighbor folks who were usually too busy working to visit.

For my family, the Practical County Fair was all about beef.

Dad's family had raised some of the best beef in Indiana for generations. The Ryan family farm, dubbed Ryansmeade by Granddad's Irish parents, sat on four hundred acres located exactly fourteen and a half miles from Nowhere. Nowhere, Indiana. Population four thousand and not really growing much. Now, I've often wondered, *Who on God's green earth names a town Nowhere?* Because Nowhere is actually somewhere. It's the county seat of Practical County, and it's right smack-dab in the middle of the flattest fields of northern Indiana.

Dad was raised here, and so was Mom. And generations of their families before them. Granddad, Dad's dad, was my only living grandparent, and he lived in the old home place right beside the pasture and about a half mile from my house. The old home place looked like something from a folk-art painting. A square, white, plain-fronted, wooden-sided farmhouse with twin chimneys on each end. Except for new paint every four years and the electric lines that linked it to the poles along the road, that house probably looked just like it did when it was built a hundred years ago. It was old. And it was big for just Granddad, but he had been born there and he'd sworn time and time again that he would die there when the good Lord had a notion to take him.

Just then Granddad stepped out onto the small back porch, slipped his stocking feet into his black rubber boots, and joined us at the pasture gate.

"Good morning," he said to all of us, calves included. "You here to pick 'em out, Libby?"

"You bet I am."

"Are you sure about this, Lib?" Dad asked. He still had that hint of doubt in his voice. As if a girl couldn't possibly fill my older brother Ronnie's shoes. Well, maybe I couldn't yet handle those big, square hay bales like Ronnie could, but I was sure I could show a steer just as good, and, I hoped, better.

"I'm sure, Dad," I told him with no hint of doubt in my voice.

Looking out over the pasture as the September morning grew into a sweltering day, I knew I had an important task ahead of me. Two of these calves would be mine; I had to be sure we had at least one winner.

I had been to the Practical County Beef Show every year for as long as I could recall, watching and cheering for Ronnie in the show ring. There was so much to take in. The exhibitors as they maneuvered their enormous animals around the ring. The judges, deep in thought as they ranked each steer in their minds. The hush that fell over the crowd just before the champion was selected. I'd seen it all from the stands, and watching my big brother show steers was thrilling. But now that I was twelve, it was my turn. At next summer's fair, it would be *me* in the show ring. And I had big plans. Not only would I prove to Dad that I could show steers, but I would show the Grand Champion steer as well.

It just made sense that a Grand Champion steer would come from Ryansmeade. Dad and Granddad were known to be two of the best cattlemen around. And though Ronnie had done well, Grand Champion, even Reserve Champion, had escaped my brother. Now that he had left for Purdue University, it would be up to me to bring the family the recognition it deserved.

Dad always said it wasn't about winning, but we all knew how it was between farmers in Practical County. The competition was tough. There were plenty of folks who knew an awful lot about raising and showing cattle. Then there were those who just thought they did. Like the Darlings.

Dad and Granddad had struck up their usual conversation.

"Had purty near an inch an' a quarter Tuesday night. How much did they get in town?"

Rainfall. You'd think it would be a springtime topic. But not for farmers. They measured rainfall on a daily basis year-round, like a supermodel measures fat grams. Honestly, I didn't really see the point in keeping such close track of either one.

I studied the group of calves until I had a good idea which two were perfect for the Practical County Fair. There were mostly Angus, I noticed, their jet-black hair smooth and shiny in the sun. Here and there I spotted a Shorthorn, with big blotches of red and white on its sides. I had to admit, they were just about the sweetest group of calves I'd ever seen. Just thinking about taking two of them home to our own barn made me eager to cut the chatter and get on with it.

Granddad seemed to read my mind.

"I'll bet you'd like to pick out your calves and take them on home, wouldn't you, Libby?" he said with a grin.

"I've got them picked out already," I told him.

"Do you, now? Well, I happen to have a couple in mind, too. Tell you what, Lib, you pick one, and then I'll pick you a champion." He winked.

"Sounds fair to me," I agreed.

"Well then, ladies first."

"Okay," I said. "How about this little guy right here?"

I pointed to the adorable Angus mix that had been sucking my fingers with the power of a vacuum cleaner. Granddad smiled and scratched the calf's black-and-white head.

"You read my mind, Libby dear. And now . . ."

Granddad's eyes scanned the lot.

"Pick me out a winner, Granddad."

"Okay, well, how 'bout that fella right back there?"

My eyes followed his pointing finger to a smaller, black calf at the back of the lot. The calf turned to glance in our direction, then turned slowly away as if to say that he wasn't very impressed with us, either.

"Looks like he's a calm one," Dad said with a nod.

Calm, sure. He wasn't skittish like some of the others. And he certainly wasn't jumpy. But was he even *breathing*?

I shot my dad a look of doubt, but he was already headed toward the stock trailer.

"Granddad?" I asked. "Are you sure about that one?"

I studied the Angus calf once again, looking for something appealing but finding nothing at all to make me want to take him home. He was a mess from the tip of his wet nose to the end of his matted, muddy tail.

Granddad's blue eyes sparkled. "Never been more sure of anything, Libby."

Just like that, it was a done deal.

TWO

— fair calves don't need names —

As we drove up the long lane to our place, we could hear both calves bellowing their displeasure at leaving the pasture.

"You're home, guys!" I shouted over the racket of their cries and the metal trailer bouncing up the gravel drive. I could hardly believe I had two of my very own animals to raise. It would be a project Dad and I could work on together. I couldn't remember ever doing anything with Dad that didn't involve Ronnie, too.

Home was a collection of buildings that surrounded a big square gravel barnyard. The barn was the center of it all, its huge black hip roof standing taller than even the tallest trees on the farm. A newer, metal machine shed stretched out along the north end of the barn, and to the south sat the old corncrib, granary, and chicken house. Our house stood tall in front of it all, a two-story yellow farmhouse, much newer than Granddad's, but an antique when compared to the houses in Nowhere that Mom had listed with the real estate agency.

"Oooh, Libby! They're so a-dor-able!" Frannie squealed as we unloaded the two calves from the trailer and into their pen. The first calf stepped with ease off of the back of the trailer, just as he had stepped up onto it at Granddad's. The second calf was much less willing to go and needed prodding.

"What are we going to name them?"

"*We* aren't going to name them anything," I reminded my little sister. "*I* am going to name them, but not until I'm good and ready."

Frannie scowled. She looked hurt. There it was again. That chubby-cheeked cherub face. Her unruly bangs had fallen over her sky blue eyes, and she used a plump fist to push them aside. Why'd she have to be so cute? I decided to humor her.

"Any ideas?"

Now that I was open to suggestions, Frannie's scowl disappeared. She had that I-thought-you'd-never-ask look on her face. It was a look that ranked somewhere between perky and disgusting.

"Yes," she said decidedly. "My grandchildren think you should call them Toto and Dorothy."

Why had I even bothered?

Frannie was a four-year-old with the vocabulary of a

forty-year-old and an imagination the size of Texas. Some kids have imaginary friends, maybe even imaginary pets. But not my little sister. No, that would be too ordinary. My sister had imaginary *grandchildren*. Two of them. Sometimes her imaginary grandchildren were amusing, but most of the time, their very existence was embarrassing.

The worst part about the grandchildren was that I never knew exactly where they were. Sometimes I would sit on them—quite by accident, I assure you—and when that happened, we'd all get to experience the wrath of Fran.

"You sat on Esmerelda Emily!"

Eventually, I learned to try to avoid sitting down when Frannie was in the room.

The calves immediately began exploring their new surroundings. I broke a bale of straw into their pen. Delighted with the fresh bedding beneath him, the black-and-white calf skittered across the barn, kicking up his hind legs and scattering the clean yellow straw. The smaller calf stood in the corner of the pen, quietly surveying his new home.

"Yippee!" Frannie cheered as she climbed another step higher on the rusty pipe gate.

"Careful there."

Dad's voice was serious, and it matched the look on his face, which was almost brown after a summer of wheat harvest and baling straw and hay. His skin showed some deep lines, mostly from the worries of farm life. Dad was all about work. Year-round, from before dawn to well into the night, Dad was either on a tractor, with the cattle, or fixing broken machinery. Not all that long ago, Dad's hair had been brown like mine, but recently the gray had begun to take over.

Ronnie had gotten Dad's tall, lanky build. My height, or lack of it, came from Mom's side of the family.

"Yeah, Frannie," I echoed Dad's warning. "You better watch your step on that gate."

But when I glanced at Dad I saw that it wasn't Frannie's climbing that had prompted his words of caution. He was looking right at me.

"Be careful there," he repeated. "Fair calves don't need names."

"Sure they do, Dad!" I protested. "We can't just go around saying, 'Here, calf,' for the rest of the year. Every barn animal has to be called *something*."

Dad was used to his own cattle, who milled around in the feedlot behind the barn or roamed in the pasture out by the woods. Hundreds of them were raised each year on the Ryan farm. Sure, a person didn't name that kind of animal. But these were bucket babies, special little guys who needed care and attention.

"Suit yourself" was all he said as he stirred powdery milk replacer into two buckets of warm water. But then he added, "Your brother never named his show cattle."

I was used to being compared with Ronnie. Dad missed him, now that he was at Purdue. I was sure of that. Dad and Ronnie used to sit at the kitchen table late into the night and plan the farm's next crop rotation, cattle sale, or machinery trade.

Humph. Well, I'm not Ronnie, I thought.

I took the first bucket. The watery milk was sweet-smelling and sticky, and the calves knew without a doubt it was feeding time. The special feeder for newborns had a soft plastic nipple attached, and the first calf nearly knocked the other over to get at it. He took the nipple without any coaxing, and I laughed as he sucked and slurped noisily. The calf gulped, tipped his head to the left, then to the right, and nearly jerked the bucket right out of my hands.

When he was finished, I had to pull back on the bucket and pry my fingers into the calf's mouth to get him to let go of the nipple. Frannie giggled at the little calf's strength.

"He eats like a pig!" she cried.

The calf tipped his head back to see if he could get anything else to eat out of my hands.

I had to agree. I looked into his wide black eyes and said, "Yes, sir, you are a little piggy!"

That was the moment Piggy acquired the perfect name, a name he would live up to with pride.

Naming the second calf wasn't quite so easy.

I got very little help when my best friend, Carol Ann, stopped by with her mom to see the new calves that evening. She opened the car door almost before her mother was completely stopped.

"Let's see these bovine beasts," she said as she marched to the barn. Always on a mission, that was Carol Ann. Her straight, dark hair was just long enough to tuck behind her ears when she wasn't wearing a trademark headband.

My family loved Carol Ann. She was great with Frannie. She had the patience that I never seemed to be able to find when I needed it. At least once a month she made Frannie laugh orange pop out her nose. Most of the other girls at school would have been disgusted, but not Carol Ann. She had half a dozen brothers and sisters, all younger, and she'd seen things worse than orange pop come out of places worse than noses.

"You need something clever, something with panache," Carol Ann said with determination as she patted the calf's soft, fuzzy neck.

"I don't even know what panache is."

I turned away and fiddled with the feed sack so she wouldn't see me roll my eyes at her big word. It would never ever occur to me to use half the words that came out of Carol Ann's mouth. I wondered if she could hear my eyes rolling in the way my voice sounded. If anyone could hear an eye-roll, it would be Carol Ann Cuthbert.

"How about Socrates? Or maybe something presidential like William? Or Walker? Or George? No, those names sound too stuffy. How about Ronald, like in Reagan?"

"Carol Ann! Ronald is my brother's name. I can't name my steer after my brother."

"Oh, yeah, that wouldn't be good."

For someone with a whole lot of brains, Carol Ann could be so absentminded sometimes.

"Oh, forget it," I said, wanting to move the conversation on to something else. "That calf will name himself sooner or later."

"You're right," Carol Ann agreed.

Carol Ann was everything you'd ever want in a friend. Honest, down-to-earth, tell-it-like-it-is people like her were hard to come by. She made me laugh, but she said I was the funny one. She was dreadfully brainy, which made us dreadfully different, but that didn't bother me most of the time. Together, Carol Ann and I had survived elementary school

17

and were ready to tackle seventh grade at Nowhere Middle School with gusto. Carol Ann would have used a different word, like *vehemence*.

Oh, and another thing. I should have known better than to ask for her assistance in naming the calf. Carol Ann's dog has a white house with his name, Phydeaux, spelled out neatly in black letters over the door. Almost no one else gets it.

THREE

— meet the darlings —

One of my favorite places on the Ryan family farm was the front porch. Our farmhouse had a porch that wrapped its way around three sides, making room for plenty of rockers, gliders, and, Frannie's favorite, the long porch swing with the flowered cushion that was just perfect for her. And Eugene. And Esmerelda Emily.

It was after supper on Sunday evening, and Mom and Dad had just settled into their own favorite chairs on the porch when a shiny red pickup came flying up the lane, sending dust from the gravel drive in all directions.

Dad stood up and let out a sigh.

"Looks like we've got company."

Sure enough, the calves had been in the barn for less

than two days before the Darlings arrived to check out their competition. There was no mistaking the candy-apple-red crew-cab truck with dualies and enough chrome to be blinding, even in the fading sunlight.

Three girls piled out of the truck and made a beeline for the barn while Mr. Darling headed up the porch steps to chat with my parents. I would have to deal with the Darling girls myself.

When I got to the barn, the sisters were already examining my new calves, whispering and pointing, especially to the smaller one.

Precious, the oldest and a senior at Nowhere High, was the first to speak, as usual.

"Nice calves, Libby," she said, her voice dripping with sarcasm. "But where are your *fair* calves?"

Now, when Mr. and Mrs. Jim Darling named their first daughter Precious everyone in town wanted to puke. I, of course, was not yet born, but I felt the exact same way once I was old enough to appreciate Precious Darling's lack of ability to live up to her name.

I never did understand how someone could give their kids names like Angel or Grace. Tell me, why would anyone do that? Isn't that just tempting fate, if there is such a thing? What happens when a kid named Angel has to go to the principal's office twice a week, or Grace constantly trips over her own two feet?

Well, it was no different with Precious, because she was anything but. Sure, she was pretty. Perfect teeth, long blond hair that she shook behind her like she was in a shampoo commercial. Indestructible hot-pink salon nails. She was gorgeous. Okay, Ronnie used to say she was "drop-dead gorgeous," but her biggest flaw was that she knew it. And she wanted to be sure everyone else did, too.

Standing there in the barn in her yellow sundress and flip-flops, Precious looked out of place. It was really hard to imagine her taking care of her own steer on the Darling farm.

"Hello," I said to all three of them. "These *are* my fair calves."

Like she didn't already know that. Please.

"Oh, really?" Precious eyeballed Piggy and his still-unnamed companion. "They're pretty scrawny, aren't they? And dirty."

Immediately I began to wish I'd talked Granddad into a different calf. I also wished I had cleaned them up a little, but Dad firmly believed they needed a few days to adjust to their new surroundings before we started working with them.

"Well, they just came in from the pasture," I tried to explain.

"Our calves came from the auction barn," Lil piped up. "They were already clean when we got them."

Yes, two years after Precious Darling was born there came another Darling baby girl. Lil. Not Lilly, not Lillian. Just Lil. The lady who typed the birth certificate nearly refused. Okay, I wasn't born yet then, either, but that was what everyone always said. Lil Darling was a carbon copy of Precious. She spent her life walking like her sister, talking like her sister, dressing like her sister, and usually going out with the guys her sister dumped. They were two of a kind, except that Precious was clearly in charge and Lil rarely had a thought of her own.

"What brings you three all the way out here?" I asked no one in particular. I was really trying to avoid making eye contact with the youngest Darling daughter, the one who was my age and was fiddling uncomfortably with her blue cotton sundress.

Her name? Ohma. No joke. The third Darling girl was named Ohma Darling. And I can tell you (this time from personal experience, because I was born in the same hospital, on the very same day) Ohma was without a doubt the least darling Darling of all.

When Ohma Darling was no more than two years old, it became obvious that she wasn't made from the same mold as her sisters. For starters, she never grew the thick, flowing, golden locks that her sisters managed to acquire. Her frizzy brown mop was unmanageable even short.

By the time Ohma started kindergarten at Nowhere Elementary, it was becoming more and more obvious that she wasn't going to have her sisters' petite build, either. She was a foot taller than the rest of our class and she was already wearing the same dresses Lil and Precious had worn in the third grade.

Ohma was definitely a different Darling. Maybe the most striking difference was her odd personality. While her sisters were chattery and giggly, Ohma said very little that wasn't an echo of what her older sisters said. And she almost never smiled. In fact, she wore a constant scowl.

"What do you think we're doing here?" Lil huffed. "We heard about your new calves."

"Yeah," grumbled Ohma. "We heard about your new calves."

How they even knew I had picked out my calves was beyond me. But life is like that in a small town. Word gets around. If you're sick, folks know all about it. If someone buys a new truck, some farm ground, or even a pair of jeans from Wal-Mart, someone somewhere in Practical County is talking about it.

"Yeah, they really don't look much like champions to me," Precious added, twirling her hair with a finger. "But then again, your brother, Ronnie, never had a champion steer, did he?"

Like you'd know a champion steer if you saw one, I thought. Every steer Ronnie ever showed was way better than anything that the Darlings had brought to the fair, and his room was filled with ribbons to prove it. I was steaming, but I didn't want Precious and her sisters to know it.

Calmly, I said, "Well, there's a lot of time between now and next summer's fair."

Stick with the facts. Granddad's advice came in handy. When you're up against someone with a lot of opinions, just stick with the facts.

Right then it didn't seem to matter much what the facts were, the Darlings were moving on, having seen what they came to see. I noticed that Precious was headed right for a clump of fresh manure.

"Be careful where you step," I warned, but it was too late.

"Eww!" Precious squealed as one flip-flop landed squarely in the pile and brown manure oozed around her bare toes. "Oh, nasty! Libby Ryan! You did that on purpose."

Right. I put that manure there just in case the Darling sisters happened to drop by unannounced.

"There's a water pump right by the door," I told her.

"Your barn is gross, Libby," Lil snapped. She was dressed exactly like her older sister, only her dress and flip-flops were lavender. "You should get one of those fork thingies and clean that up."

Lil's suggestion made me furious, knowing that she had spent little, if any, time with a pitchfork in her hands. Obviously, she didn't even know what it was called.

I left the small mess on the barn floor. It was a tiny bit satisfying just knowing how much the Darling girls wanted it gone. Precious had returned, hopping on one foot and shaking a water-soaked flip-flop in the air.

Having apparently seen enough of the inside of our barn, Precious waved a perfectly manicured hand and announced, "Okay, well, we're going now."

Lil, who had been busy shooing flies away from her face, snapped quickly to attention at her sister's command.

"Yes, we are going now."

Ohma grunted in agreement and started for the barnyard.

"Your calves are"—Precious hesitated, searching for a word—"okay."

That might have been the end of it if Lil had been able to hold her tongue.

"Yeah, they're okay. But just wait until you see our calves. This year we—"

She never got a chance to finish. Precious grabbed her sister by the elbow and yanked her out of the barn, hushing her all the way to their truck.

24

Later, I mulled over the events of the evening. Why were the Darlings so interested in seeing my calves? When Ronnie showed cattle, the Darlings never paid much attention to his animals. Dad said it was likely the girls' father who had prompted the visit. Mr. Jim Darling wanted two things in life: sons and a Grand Champion steer. Well, he hadn't gotten the sons, but he had never given up on the Grand Champion steer. Trouble was, he'd never have one if his daughters didn't learn to work a whole lot harder on their livestock projects.

It would probably seem odd that the Darling girls showed steers in the first place, except that showing was practically a requirement of farm kids in Practical County. Those girls weren't exactly the types to get their hands dirty doing anything, but year after year, Precious and Lil loaded their fancy livestock trailer with some pretty scruffy-looking steers. They never were much of a threat to Ronnie. Just because their father made them show didn't mean they liked it, and it sure didn't mean they were any good at it.

The Darling girls did share one claim to fame (besides their terribly original names). What they lacked in steer-raising skills, they made up for in the Practical County Beef Princess pageant. Yes, they were the perennial princesses of beef. For the past four years, the coveted title of Beef Princess had gone to a Darling. Precious held a county record for beef royalty, having won the title three years in a row. After beating her older sister in what turned out to be a knock-down, drag-out competition last year, Lil was this year's reigning Princess. And Ohma would have been a shoo-in as her successor if it weren't for Ohma's obvious lack of queenlike qualities. No doubt, when it came to representing roast, the Darling daughters reigned.

But who could even begin to speculate whether the Darlings could dominate the Beef Princess pageant next summer? And what was it that Precious didn't want Lil to say about their own calves? Surely they didn't believe they had calves any better than those raised at Ryansmeade. Judging from their odd behavior in the barn, I began to wonder if they weren't planning something entirely different.

FOUR

— stubborn as a mule —

"How are Porky and his friend?" Mom asked me, the phone propped between her ear and her shoulder as she stirred something on the stove. Only her eyes lifted when I walked into the kitchen. If she had lifted her head, the phone would have slipped into boiling whatever.

"Piggy, Mom," I corrected. "His name is Piggy."

The kitchen was the center of activity in our house. It had an enormous oak table with long wooden benches on each side, big enough for a family twice the size of ours. When we didn't fill it with dinner guests—Granddad was a nightly regular—one end remained covered with homework, land maps, or blueprints from Mom's latest real estate sale.

Mom was into paint. Red Scarf Red in the bathroom. Summer Sky Blue in the laundry room. Dad said she got too many ideas from selling new houses in Nowhere, but every few years she painted a different room and last summer it had been the kitchen's turn. The result was Fresh Pear Green on the walls, with sunny yellow curtains and place mats. With the old white cupboards and the worn hardwood floor, even Dad had to admit the lively combination made the kitchen a fun place to hang out.

"Yes, I'm here, Roger," Mom said into the phone. It was Roger, her boss, and I knew it wouldn't be a quick conversation. Mom glanced up at me again and gave me the we-can-talk-later look. The trouble with we-can-talk-later was that later usually came when there was a client on the line, a fax coming in, or Frannie dramatically making a demand that was far more urgent than anything I could possibly have to say.

The calves had been at the farm less than a week, and it was obvious that Mom's interest in them was going to be pretty much limited to trying to remember their names and snapping photos of us with them while saying things like "Can't you make Porky look *this* way?"

That was just Mom. Busy Mom. She was short, like me, with light brown, curly hair and energy to burn. Mom was always on the go. She had her real estate work, she had her volunteer work at the food pantry, she had the house, the laundry, and heaven knows she had Frannie. What she didn't have was much time for whatever was happening in the barn.

No, it really didn't surprise me one bit that this calf

thing would be a Dad thing, not a Mom thing. And that was okay with me. I'd been waiting for my turn to share some of Dad's time. Ronnie usually did all the Dad things, and Mom took care of us girls. But the day after Ronnie had gone off to college at the end of the summer, I heard Dad tell Mom that he was heading to a livestock auction over in Rochester.

"Sure wish Ronnie could go," he had said. "It ought to be a good sale."

He'd never taken me to one of the auctions. I stepped into the room.

"I'll go," I offered.

"No, Libby, I don't think so." He shook his head. "You'd just be bored, kiddo."

I was trying to think of reasons why he should take me, but he was in a hurry. I'd missed my chance. Maybe with my calves I could prove to him that I could do all the things he used to do with Ronnie.

Mom continued to talk into the phone while silently shooing Frannie away as if she were an oversized fly. And what a colorful oversized fly Frannie was that day! Finger paint to her elbows, she was following Mom around the kitchen, asking if blue and red would still make purple if you also added green. Judging from the purplish black paint on her arms, it was a question Frannie already knew the answer to. Mom made the not-now face while nodding and giving an occasional "ummm-hmmm" into the phone.

I nearly made it to the garage door, and I would have succeeded in escaping completely if I hadn't committed one fatal mistake. I looked once more in Mom's direction.

I should have known better. She caught me with that desperate help-your-sister-*pleeeeease* look. I was nailed.

I turned to Frannie and put on my helpful-big-sister smile.

"That is an extraordinary color you're using, Fran. Would you like me to help you wash your hands?"

"*Excuse me. . . .*" She inhaled as she said it, like a pitcher winding up for a fastball.

I knew I should have bolted for the door when I had the chance.

She put her hands on her hips, paint and all, and stated, "You are *not* in this con-per-sation!"

She whirled away from me as Mom made her escape into the living room still ummm-hmmming into the cordless phone.

"Frannie, if you'll just let me help—"

"*We* don't want *you*. *We* want *Mom*."

"We?"

"Yes, *we*. Can't you see Eugene standing right there beside you?"

I looked at the empty space around me.

"Frannie, listen, you're going to have to—"

"*Ahhhh!*"

"Stop screaming, Frannie."

"But Esmerelda Emily just about touched you with green paint all over her hands!"

Okay, that was it. One obnoxious four-year-old was enough, but these grandchildren she'd invented were driving me nuts!

"Fine, then," I told her. "You and your grandchildren

will just have to wait for Mom. But don't touch anything with those messy hands. Any of you!"

"We won't," Frannie answered as she climbed up on the wooden bench, grasping the edge of the table with two plump purple hands.

I had done my part to the best of my ability, considering whom I was dealing with, and I headed out through the garage, across the barnyard, and into the barn. Like the front porch on the house, the barn was one of my favorite places on the farm. Granddad always said a man can judge a farm by its barn. A sturdy, well-kept barn meant a good farmer lived and worked there, he said, and for the most part, his observation held true. White with a black hip roof, our barn has stood unchanged for more than seventy years.

Granddad would say, "Yup, they just don't make 'em like this anymore."

He was right. If it looked big from the outside, the barn was enormous on the inside. The huge, rounded roof arched what seemed like a mile overhead. The two mows, one for straw and one for hay, were nearly full this time of year, giving the place a fresh smell strong enough to overpower the damp manure from the stalls below.

Piggy ran to the gate to greet me.

"Hi there, fella," I cooed to him as I scratched behind both his ears. He lifted his head and extended his long tongue to grab hold of my coat sleeve. He had grown already and was starting to lose his fuzzy baby coat.

"You hungry again?"

The second calf stayed at the far end of the pen. He never took his eyes off me as I walked around the barn, sweeping the floor and pumping fresh water from the hydrant. He never flinched, even as I talked to him.

"We've got to come up with a name for you, fella. We can't just call you 'the other calf' forever, you know."

I threw one leg over the gate and my boot squished into the brown mixture of manure and straw. Piggy nuzzled my hand and licked my palm, hoping, I was sure, to find it filled with grain.

"Sorry, Pig." I scratched his forehead and gently moved him aside. "I need to have a chat with this guy over here."

To my complete amazement, the other calf didn't startle or try to escape my presence as I approached. In fact, he stood perfectly still, allowing me to run my hands along his back and rub behind his ears.

"There now," I told him. "You're not unfriendly at all. You're just shy, aren't you, little guy?"

Testing my luck, I reached for the rope halter hanging on a nail over the feed bunk. Slowly, carefully, I turned with the slightest of movements, fearing I'd spook him if I moved too fast. I kept one hand running evenly along his shoulder and back while I carefully slipped his nose into the halter. The calf turned his head from one side to the other but didn't move his feet at all.

"Now we're getting somewhere." I smiled at him as the halter slid easily over his ears and into position.

The calf turned his shiny black head toward me as I spoke. That was when I noticed his deep blue eyes. They were so blue, I had to look twice. He blinked his long, wispy lashes, again revealing the dark blue summer-night color of his eyes.

For a moment, I was sorry for misjudging him. For an instant my heart went out to this sweet, gentle animal standing so calmly before me.

But only for an instant.

When I gently pulled on the rope halter to move forward, the calf did not budge.

"Come on," I coaxed. "Come on."

I tugged lightly.

"Come on, sweetie." I pulled a little harder.

Nothing. I tugged at the halter and nudged his shoulder with mine.

"Let's go," I said, a little more loudly.

Still not a step. It was as if his feet were glued to the straw.

"All right," I nearly shouted. *"Come on!"*

I yanked. Hard. By now the animal was moving. *Backward*. He stretched his neck against the pull of the halter, and without a moment's notice, he jerked his head. I was caught off guard. The rope slid from my fingers and I landed on my butt in the slick straw. As the wet manure seeped up and soaked my jeans, the calf turned his head again to one side and blinked an innocent blue eye.

"You," I sputtered. "You are as stubborn as a mule."

From the straw mow far above came a familiar giggle.

"Mule! Hey, Muley-Muley-Mule! Let's call him Mule!"

I closed my eyes as my elbows sank deeper into the mucky straw. How did that child always manage to be everywhere all the time?

FIVE

— autumn surprise —

As September fell away into October, Dad's usual preoccupation with work turned to obsession with the harried task of harvest. It'd be harder on both Dad and Granddad this year with Ronnie out of the daily picture. He'd been a big help during high school, and like most farm boys, he had been allowed to take two or three days off school when harvesttime was at its busiest.

The soybeans ripened first, changing almost overnight from huge green bushes to skinny dry stalks loaded with fuzzy brown pods ready to burst at the seams. The corn quickly followed, providing truckloads of hard yellow kernels to fill the grain bins and more work than there were days in November.

Dad's modern machinery, like the enormous John Deere combine, made harvest easier, faster, and safer than it had been in Granddad's day. But the technology that made farming more efficient had also changed the face of the family farm. I'd heard it discussed over and over again on Friday afternoons at Cuthbert's Hardware.

Nowhere was one of the few towns that still had an old-fashioned hardware store, complete with a long counter and a row of wooden stools that tended to attract the farmers on rainy days or even sunny ones in the wintertime. Carol Ann's father owned it, and it had been in his family for generations. When Carol Ann and I were little, we used to wander behind the counter and open the hundreds of little wooden drawers full of nuts and bolts and screws. The hardware store always smelled exactly the same. A combination of old wood, new tools, leather, and aftershave. The smell never changed, and neither did the conversation.

"The only way to do it is to do it big," Mr. Parker, the retired high school vocational agriculture teacher, would say, and others would always agree.

"Yep, there just ain't no way the little guy can make a living farming." Mr. Cuthbert would nod.

"Some guys gotta take factory jobs to support their hobby!"

This comment from old Grove Everett brought a chuckle from Dad and the others.

But fall meant that the only folks hanging around at Cuthbert's Hardware were the old-timers, too old to do the work but still sharp enough to talk about how the next generation ought to be doing it. Granddad hadn't reached that point quite yet. Ronnie's absence meant that he was back behind the wheel of a tractor, a duty that prompted him to suddenly behave as if he were half his age, whooping and hollering as he drove by, honking the horn just to see if it still worked. It would be Thanksgiving before Ronnie would make the trip home from Purdue, and by then, weather permitting, all the crops would be in.

I wanted to do my part, so I told Dad I would take care of barn chores by myself before and after school. Early in the fall, when the school bus dropped me off at the end of the lane, I would find Frannie and her grandchildren waiting on the front porch. She begged to help, so I gave her, or should I say *them*, the job of feeding the numerous barn cats. In the mudroom we kept a collection of holey jeans, old sweatshirts, and anything else that we wouldn't want to be seen in at school. These were dubbed "barn clothes," and that was where Frannie and I would change before going out to tackle the evening chores together.

Frannie was fascinated with the barn cats. To me, they were ever-present mouse chasers, all looking pretty much the same, rather nondescript black and gray tiger cats. But to Frannie, each was unique, and each deserved a special name.

In September she named them all after food. There was Pickle, and Lemonade, and Sugar, and Ice Cream. She named one Macaroni and another Cheese, and she tried to make them stand together at all times. That resulted in at least one scratch.

But by mid-October it had turned rainy, and Frannie made fewer trips to the barn with me.

"Eugene and Esmerelda Emily aren't feeling well," she

explained as I pulled an old gray sweatshirt over my head one day after school. "They should not be out in this mis-er-ble weather, so I think I will stay inside to take care of them."

How convenient, I thought.

The wet ground conditions kept Dad and Granddad out of the field and chomping at the bit for more than two weeks. The bad weather was delaying harvest.

Mom cooked extra-nice meals those weeks. Comfort food, she called it, knowing Dad was worried about the crops. The lines on his face grew deeper with each soggy day that passed. Granddad, on the other hand, remained light-hearted.

"I've seen wet Octobers before," he said. "Just be glad it ain't snow! I've seen that before, too!"

In northern Indiana, snow in October wasn't impossible.

By the end of the month, the rain did stop, and though it was chilly, the afternoon sun dried out the fields enough that harvest could resume. It meant the farmers would have to go at full speed to get finished.

Mule and Piggy knew just when to expect me each morning and night. Even Mule ambled over to the feed bunk to greet me when I slid the barn doors open one Friday evening. Alone in the barn, I spoke to them freely.

"Hi, guys. How's it going today?"

I talked to them while I mixed their feed, telling them the news of the day.

"Mom has two new listings on houses in Nowhere," I told Piggy, who listened intently, or maybe he was just wait-ing for me to pour the grain into the feed bunk. He watched

37

me closely as I explained how Dad and Granddad would be working at breakneck speed to bring in the last of the corn over the weekend.

"And listen to this," I told both steers, who now stood with heads between the gates, eyeing the bucket in my hand. "Carol Ann and I have just been made partners for our science project, and you don't even know what a huge relief that is, because, besides Carol Ann and me, there were only Karen Elliott and Ohma Darling left for Mr. Collins to pair up. Boy, when he said my name, I held my breath and didn't let it out until he said Carol Ann's. Poor Karen. I'm sure Ohma is going to be nearly impossible to work with."

Always hungry, Piggy paced restlessly while I chatted. Eventually, he nuzzled up to me while I talked, his square black nose soft and wet. He put his head under my arm, waving his furry ear in my face.

"Aw, Pig, I love you, too," I told him. His fuzzy warmth made him so cuddly, and his impatience to be fed was endearing.

Mule, on the other hand, stood still. Was he listening? Maybe, I decided, but it was unlikely. He seemed way too self-absorbed to care about my day.

When I tipped the grain bucket so its contents spilled out into the feed bunk, both animals started eating like they hadn't seen grain for days.

"Liiiiibbyyyy!"

Frannie's voice sang out from the barnyard. Had she changed her mind about coming out to do chores? I walked to the barn doors.

Frannie was alone, or at least without visible company. She was grinning her I-know-something-you-don't grin.

"Guess who's here?" She beamed.

I looked around, seeing no one.

"I don't know, Frannie. Eugene?"

Frannie shook her head. "Nope. Someone bigger."

"Granddad?"

"Nope," came the giggled reply.

"Frannie, really, is it someone invisible? Because . . ."

I stopped as the side door to the house opened and out stepped Ronnie, sliding his arms into a flannel jacket while he crunched a Golden Delicious apple he'd no doubt snatched from the kitchen counter.

"*Ronnie!*"

I ran across the gravel barnyard and threw myself right into his arms. The apple core flew straight up in the air, landing in the yard by his feet.

"Whoa, there, Libby! What a welcome! Good thing I was done with that apple."

His hearty laugh sounded more like Granddad's than I had ever noticed before, and I was sure he was taller than he had been in August.

It had only been two months since we'd taken Ronnie and half of his belongings to a tiny dorm room at Purdue, but it felt like two years. I'd wondered then how a farm boy like Ronnie, so used to the wide-open spaces of Ryansmeade, would survive dormitory life. And here he was back home long before the end of the semester.

"Wait a minute. What are you doing here?" I asked,

suddenly worried that he'd changed his mind about college. "Did you . . ."

The broad smile never left his face.

"No, Libby, I didn't quit school. I knew Dad and Grand-dad were way behind schedule with harvest. A guy from the third floor was going home to Wabash for the weekend. He offered me a ride, and here I am. Dad says we'll get all the corn in now for sure."

I was relieved that Ronnie was okay with school. Going to Purdue had been a dream of Ronnie's since he was my age. But now, I had so much to tell him. And show him.

"You have to see Mule and Piggy. Do you have time? Real quick, before Granddad gets back with the next load of corn?"

"Sure, Lib, let's see these prize calves."

I pulled him with me into the barn, and Frannie followed, staring up at her big brother, quieter than she'd been in ages.

As Ronnie looked the calves over, I explained to him about how Piggy had pretty much picked me that morning at Granddad's pasture. I told him how Piggy had sucked and slobbered on my fingers and then had earned his name and lived up to it ever since. When I tried to introduce Mule, he turned his head away and ignored Ronnie.

"That one," I told him, "that one is stubborn, and I don't know what I'm going to do with him."

Ronnie surveyed Mule while Piggy nuzzled his jacket pockets for grain.

"Well, I don't know, Lib. They both look like show

calves to me. I'd have a tough time deciding which one to take to the Practical County Fair."

"Oh," I said confidently, "I know who's going and who's staying."

Ronnie laughed.

"Don't be too quick to decide. A lot can happen over a winter. And you need to take the best one. You know I never got Champion. So if Ryansmeade is ever going to get it, it'll be up to you, Lib."

Thanks for the reminder, big brother, I thought.

"There's a lot of competition in Practical County," I reminded him. "Maybe more than you had in the past."

Ronnie gave me the oh-really raised-eyebrow look, and I told him about the Darling sisters' unusual September visit.

"It was so strange, Ronnie. Precious, Lil, and Ohma never showed much interest in their own cattle. Why are they suddenly interested in mine?"

"Maybe they think they've got a winner this year," Ronnie suggested, his voice serious until a playful smile spread across his face.

We both burst into laughter, knowing that in all the years Ronnie had shown cattle against them, nothing had come out of Darling Farms worth turning a judge's head even for a second.

A rumble in the barnyard told us that Granddad was back with a hopper wagon of corn to unload, and Ronnie hurried to take his place behind the wheel of the tractor. Just before he left the barn, he turned.

"Nice calves, Lib."

His words brought a smile to my face that stayed while I finished up the chores. Even if Dad hadn't noticed that I was capable of filling Ronnie's big shoes, Ronnie had. It was a new feeling I had, this full and happy feeling, one that I later recognized as pride. I'd been proud before. Of myself. Like when I pulled off a B+ on the toughest science test ever given. But this was different. I was proud of Piggy. I was proud like I'd been of Frannie when she started saying her first words. (Of course, that was a long time ago and given the fact that she hadn't stopped talking since, I'd pretty much forgotten how excited we all were when she'd first started.)

But Piggy hadn't *done* anything. Nothing spectacular or out of the ordinary, I mean. At least not yet. He ate, he slept, he piled up manure for me to scoop out of his pen. Not much to be proud of there, right? Even so, I *was* proud of him in a way I couldn't explain.

SIX

— soup for thanksgiving —

There are some Ryan family traditions that are so certain you can count on them like you can count on the leaves to fall from the trees in autumn. No matter what. Like filling the fourth pew on the right-hand side at Nowhere Community Church each Sunday morning. Like opening Christmas presents in alphabetical order. And spending Thanksgiving Thursday at the soup kitchen in Indianapolis.

It began before Frannie was born. Mom, who started the food pantry in Nowhere, got a group of local folks together to help at an Indianapolis soup kitchen on Thanksgiving Day. Now several families from Practical County could be found working there each year. Mom always said, "There's no better way to be thankful than to spend the day serving those who have less to be thankful for."

I was about six years old the first time I made the Thanksgiving drive to the city with Mom, Dad, and Ronnie. All I really remember about that first trip was the people. There were so many. More people than at church on Sunday morning. More people than I'd seen at the Practical County Fair. The city and the soup kitchen were filled with the kinds of people you just don't see in Practical County. Some were alone, and some in large families. Some wore clothes my mother would have said were too old or torn even for the barn. And some, I remember from that first year, when I hid behind Mom's legs, talked loudly to no one at all, and I was scared. I watched them go through the line and I whispered, "Happy Thanksgiving."

So, every year, while most of the rest of Nowhere sat down to a traditional Thanksgiving dinner, the Ryan clan headed south on I-69 and into Indianapolis. This year I had asked Carol Ann to join us for what always promised to be a memorable adventure. Who could have known how very unforgettable this year's trip would be?

We left the farm before daylight, so I had to do the morning feeding in the dark. Mule and Piggy, both bedded down in the warm straw, turned to see who was intruding as I switched on the dim yellow barn light. Neither calf budged as they watched me pour grain into the feed bunk and scatter hay over the top. It was too early for even Piggy's voracious appetite.

"Have a good day, boys!" I told them as I turned off the light.

Most of the ride to the city was quiet, with Frannie dozing the entire way. By the time we pulled into the soup kitchen parking lot, the sun was already shining and people were beginning to form a line along the sidewalk and around the corner of the building. It was a chilly morning, and though Indiana had yet to see the first flake, a light dusting of snow was expected by Friday.

The soup kitchen was actually an old school that had been converted into a homeless shelter. The cafeteria was used to feed the people who stopped by daily. But to make room for the Thanksgiving crowd, the gymnasium was used. Long rows of tables were covered in white plastic with fake leaves in red, yellow, and orange scattered down the center. A miniature pumpkin with a Magic Marker face sat in the middle of each table. It was just festive enough that a person could overlook that the white walls were cracked and peeling and the ceiling tiles were water stained.

The kitchen itself was bustling with volunteers who'd already spent hours making huge pots of turkey noodle soup, piling sandwich bread high with turkey and roast beef, and pulling piping-hot pumpkin pies from enormous ovens. Though the meal lacked some of the trimmings of a traditional Thanksgiving dinner and it was served on paper plates with plastic forks, it was so feastlike and special that everyone who came felt important and satisfied.

Mom greeted several friends and neighbors from back home. Karen Elliott from science class and her parents were there. I noticed two boys from school, too.

"Ronnie, you and Dad go over and see if you can help in the back," Mom directed. "Granddad and I will cut pies for a while. Libby, it looks like they need people to ladle out soup. Why don't you and Carol Ann go do that. And keep Frannie with you. She can, um . . ."

Mom stopped and looked at Frannie, who had donned a black-and-white paper pilgrim hat she had no doubt made at preschool and stashed in the van for such an occasion as this. Frannie grinned.

"I can carry the soup."

"*No!*" came a chorus of voices in perfect unison.

"You, dear, can be a *hopper*," Mom said, emphasizing the word *hopper* to clue Frannie in on the importance of the job. "You can go around this whole big room and ask our guests if they need anything, such as a fork or a napkin or another dinner roll."

Frannie's eyes went up into her head.

"That's not a hopper, Mom. That's a *waitress!*"

We all laughed and took our places as the line we'd seen outdoors began to stream into the large gymnasium turned dining room. Carol Ann and I were filling bowls of steaming turkey noodle soup as fast as folks were taking them. We would empty one large pot and Ronnie would be waiting behind us with the next.

Frannie took her hopper-waitress role quite seriously, flitting around the room, her pilgrim hat bobbing up and down in the crowd. She wiped chairs and threw away paper plates when people left, to be ready for the next guest who would sit down. I watched her take the hand of one particularly frail older woman in a ratty brown coat and lead her to an empty seat. I was proud of Frannie. She was doing well and making very little noise at the same time.

Carol Ann and I barely had time to talk as the seemingly endless line of people shuffled by. Some of the guests smiled and spoke, some offered words of gratitude, and some just gave an appreciative nod in our direction. One woman, a mom with four small children tagging along behind her, smiled and said nothing, but her eyes were quickly filling with tears as she took the soup and led her family to a table. I wondered where the young mother's parents were, and why those children didn't have aunts and uncles and grand-parents to care for them and their mom. It wasn't that there weren't poor folks back home; it was just that in Practical County, families took care of one another. In the city, every-thing seemed so different.

After about two hours had passed, the soup kitchen manager came over to us.

"You girls ready for a little break?" he asked.

"Sure," we both agreed. I was getting thirsty.

"Well, some more girls just arrived, and I believe they're ready to get to work," he said, motioning toward the door.

I glanced toward the entrance of the gymnasium and my jaw nearly dropped into the ladle I was holding.

"Carol Ann, look!"

I nudged my friend, who gasped when she saw who was coming our way.

"The Darlings?" she whispered. "In a soup kitchen?"

I couldn't believe my eyes. Sure enough, there stood Pre-cious, Lil, and Ohma, each one overdressed for the occasion and looking very out of place.

They ambled over, staring as if they'd never seen a room full of hungry, homeless people. But then again, I was willing to bet that they never *had* seen a room full of hungry, home-less people.

Carol Ann spoke first, keeping the sarcasm in her voice to a minimum.

"Well, I see you came to help with Thanksgiving dinner. How nice of you girls!"

"What are you doing here?" I added rather bluntly. I was intensely curious to find out what could possibly have brought the Darlings here, of all places.

Lil tugged nervously at her miniskirt, her glittery nails sparkling.

"It wasn't our idea," she started. "We certainly—"

She ended abruptly as her older sister's elbow jabbed her rib cage with such force that she teetered backward on her high heels.

"We certainly are happy to help wherever we can."

Precious finished her sister's sentence, flashing a smile so fake it looked like it might fall off and shatter on the wooden floor. Lil gave her sister a stupid look.

"What about Mr.—"

This time Precious nearly knocked Lil flat as she stepped in front of her.

"Mr. What's-his-name from the soup kitchen wants us to take over here, so you two *losers* can go now," she hissed.

"Yeah, you two *losers* can go now," Ohma grumbled. Her too-tight dress and too-small heels must have been getting to her.

Carol Ann removed her apron and handed it to Precious.

"Here." She grinned. "You'll be needing this."

I passed my own apron off to Lil, who frowned, still rubbing her rib cage and looking baffled at her older sister.

We got out of there as fast as we could and headed for the volunteers' break room, where we could enjoy our own lunches.

"That was really weird," I said, crumbling saltines into my soup bowl.

"No kidding!" Carol Ann agreed.

"Can you imagine Precious Darling working on a holiday?"

"Can you imagine *any* Darling working on *any* day?"

Carol Ann had a point. There had to be some reason why the Darling trio was there. And it seemed that Lil might have been about to spill the beans before Precious had stepped in.

After we finished eating, we decided we'd better return to our posts. If only we'd left a minute sooner, we might have been able to avoid what happened next. But we were too late to prevent the Thanksgiving mishap that would without a doubt be discussed in the Ryan household for years to come.

It happened like this. Carol Ann and I stepped into the gymnasium just in time to see a black-and-white paper pilgrim hat disappear beneath a table. At the very same moment, I caught sight of Precious Darling, a tray of soup bowls balanced on one hand, turning on her high heels down the next aisle. One quick glance at Carol Ann and I knew that she and I were thinking the same thing. Frannie and Precious were on a collision course.

Carol Ann and I both scrambled to prevent the

inevitable. But when the pilgrim waitress-hopper popped out shouting "Happy Thanksgiving!" her tiny paper-covered head came up squarely on the bottom of Precious Darling's tray. The soup bowls, six of them in all, teetered on the tray, and Precious teetered on her spike-heeled shoes. The balancing act by Precious Darling was nothing less than miraculous, and by the time Carol Ann and I came to a screeching halt just inches in front of her, the tray and the bowls and even Precious had recovered from the jolt without a drop of soup spilled.

A terrified Frannie ducked back under the table. Carol Ann and I breathed a huge sigh of relief. That was when I saw the look on Precious's face change from one of surprise to one of deceit.

"Oh no!" she screamed feebly as she flipped the tray forward. All at once, six bowls of turkey noodle soup came flying at Carol Ann and me. In a split second, broth and noodles covered my sweater, my jeans, and my hair. I turned to Carol Ann. A noodle was sticking to one side of her shocked face.

I stood there in stunned silence for a second, thinking that Precious could sink no lower, when I heard:

"You stupid brat!" Precious yelled at Frannie. "You ran right into me!"

Frannie, who had managed to avoid getting soaked with soup, began to sob. She was trying her best to apologize through her tears.

"I'm sor . . . sor . . . sorry!" she wailed.

How dare Precious blame Frannie for what had

happened! Precious had dumped that tray on purpose. I'd seen the whole thing.

"No, no, Frannie," I tried to console her as the broth trickled into my shoes. "It's not your fault, honey."

Frannie broke into a fresh round of sobs, and I stood up, trying to find words strong enough to express my disgust at Precious Darling. I was opening my mouth to let her have it when I felt a hand on my shoulder.

"My goodness, what a mess we have here," Granddad said, holding out a damp rag and a stack of paper towels.

"Why, thank you, Mr. Ryan," Precious said sweetly, taking the paper towels from him. "Your granddaughter is quite the ornery one, isn't she?"

She glanced at her feet and frowned.

"Oh, look, I need to go clean off these leather shoes. It seems they got a bit of soup on them."

I saw her join her sisters, and the three of them disappeared laughing into the kitchen.

Carol Ann and I cleaned up the floor and the tables. Slowly, after what seemed like a very long minute of stunned silence, the hum of voices and clanking of metal chairs returned.

Mom took an unusually quiet Frannie to help pass out sandwiches, and Carol Ann and I finally went to the bathroom to try our best to clean ourselves up. The warm soup had cooled into a pale yellow scum that clung to our arms and faces. Bending over the sink, we used soap and paper towels to rinse off. With no change of clothes, we peeled off our sweaters and discovered that our T-shirts had been spared the worst of the mess. We used water and the bathroom's hand dryers to take some of the soup out of our hair.

As we stood picking noodles out of each other's hair, Carol Ann burst into laughter.

"It's not funny," I told her, still fuming. "Didn't you see how Precious tipped that tray on purpose?"

"I know." Carol Ann grinned. "But I can't help it. I never thought I'd come here on Thanksgiving Day and pick noodles out of your hair."

I smiled. Carol Ann always had a way of making any situation a little lighter.

"No kidding. I just hope we don't meet a hungry dog in the parking lot," I added.

Carol Ann and I giggled at the thought. From somewhere in the bathroom, I thought I heard a familiar grunt.

"Shhh." I motioned to Carol Ann. A pair of chubby-toed feet under the last stall belonged without doubt to Ohma Darling. Without another word, we left the restroom.

"Great," Carol Ann said sarcastically as we returned to the kitchen to see what we could do to help. "We've got the oldest Darling throwing food at us and the youngest spying on us."

Back in the kitchen, we were relieved to find that the Darlings were nowhere in sight.

But Karen Elliott was there, and she smiled when she saw us coming.

"Wow, that was some show!" She grinned.

"Oh, there was a lot of acting going on, that's for sure," I told her.

"What do you mean?" she asked.

Carol Ann filled Karen in on how Precious had spilled the tray on purpose.

"Only she would have the nerve to do something so mean," said Karen, shaking her head.

"Still, I feel partly responsible," I told her as I dipped the ladle into the steaming pot. "My mom told me to keep Frannie with me, and I completely forgot about her when Carol Ann and I took our break."

"Well, those Darlings have been trouble for years. At least someone is finally catching on to their deceitfulness," Karen said.

"Catching on?" Carol Ann repeated.

Karen looked around, then said in a hushed voice, "They are here today doing mandatory community service. You don't think they'd spend a single day in a soup kitchen unless they had to, do you?"

"Of course not, but why?" I asked. "What did they do?"

"Well"—Karen, who was soft-spoken anyway, was nearly whispering—"I heard that they got caught cheating."

"*All* of them? At once?" Carol Ann nearly shrieked.

"Shhh!" Karen continued. "I guess what happened is that Ohma turned in a history paper that Lil had turned in a few years ago. And when Principal Gregory checked into it, it was the same paper Precious had turned in the year before."

"No way! Only the Darlings would be arrogant enough to think a trick like that would actually work." Carol Ann rolled her eyes.

My hardworking best friend was particularly disgusted by cheating. Her own flawless academic record was something she had earned, and it burned her that some people tried to achieve the same dishonestly.

We stayed there dishing out soup with Karen until evening, when the last family was served. We saw the Darling sisters once more, each with a broom in her hand and no sign of the smugness from earlier in the day.

It was just as we were leaving, heading back to the van in the parking lot, when Ronnie noticed Mr. Gregory, the principal of Nowhere High School.

"Ronald Ryan!" Mr. Gregory beamed at the sight of one of his favorite graduates. "How's Purdue treating you?"

"Real fine, sir. I'm spending the holiday weekend with my family."

They shook hands like two businessmen.

"Nice to see you, young man."

Mr. Gregory nodded to my parents and Granddad, and they stood chatting for a few minutes.

"It's good to see you folks here. I know this has been a family tradition for the Ryans for years."

My parents and Mr. Gregory exchanged a few more words and then he excused himself. As we pulled out of the parking lot, I saw three very tired-looking Darlings getting into Mr. Gregory's car. What Karen had heard was true.

On the way home, while Frannie slept and Mom popped in a Christmas CD (right after Thanksgiving, Mom always broke out the carols), I replayed the whole soup catastrophe in my head again, thinking of Precious's shocked face when her whole tray tottered and then the calculating look that spread across it the moment she decided to dump the tray anyway. I thought of the way she had blamed poor Frannie, and I wished I had hauled off and hit her. Well, not really, I guess. But it sure didn't seem fair that she and her sisters had gone to Indianapolis because they were caught cheating and Carol Ann and I were the ones who left smelling like turkey.

SEVEN

— christmas at ryansmeade —

If the Ryan family Thanksgiving lacked something in the tradition department, Christmas more than made up for it. The entire month of December absolutely dripped with holiday cheer, Mom made sure of that.

On Christmas morning, Mom was practically goofy with excitement. She was temporarily free from the real estate business, which pretty much came to a halt every December. Who wants to buy or sell a house in the middle of the holidays?

Ronnie was home again. After Thanksgiving he had returned to school to take first-semester finals, and now he would be at Ryansmeade until the first of the year. I had so much I wanted to ask him about the calves. I was sure he'd agree that Piggy was just about perfect.

Earlier, Dad, Granddad, and Ronnie had gone out to the pasture to check the cattle. I was itching to go along, but Dad said Mom would need my help in the kitchen. He was right, of course: there was a huge dinner to prepare, and Frannie's assistance could only marginally be considered help. Still, I would have liked to join the guys outdoors.

The kitchen was festive, dressed in its holiday décor. Holly garland with tiny red plastic berries was strung over the top of the cabinets. It mingled with tiny white twinkle lights, making the room sparkle. A rosy-cheeked Santa stood in the corner by the back door, ready to greet visitors with a hearty "Ho ho ho." The CD player on the counter belted out one holiday classic after another.

In the dining room, the Christmas village that Mom had collected since she and Dad got married was spread out in front of the window, complete with fake snow and real lights in the miniature lampposts. I could spend hours staring at it, my eyes following the snowy sidewalks to one tiny building after another.

Then there was the table. Three hundred and sixty-four days a year, our dining table looked plain, almost primitive with its long benches. But on Christmas Day, Mom turned it into something from a fancy-living magazine. Grandma's bone china was the center of each place at the table, framed by silver that actually had to be polished, and topped off with linen napkins tied with huge silver bows. Mom always sighed when she set out Grandma's china. Grandma had been gone for years. I don't remember much about her at all, except that she smelled like dime-store perfume and she always had gum in her purse. All of the fancy china looked perfect on Mom's cranberry-red tablecloth. It almost looked too pretty to touch.

Frannie was busy making name cards for each place at the table.

"How do you spell 'Esmerelda Emily'?"

Mom had allowed Frannie to set two places at a small table in the corner of the dining room for the grandchildren. I didn't have a clue why Mom encouraged Frannie's nonsense.

"Sound it out, Frannie," I told her.

"Libby, hel-lo! I'm *four*!" came Frannie's emphatic reply.

"And what a precocious four you are," I said with a smile. "Sound it out."

I heard a disgusted grunt from Frannie's direction.

With the roast out of the oven, Mom popped in her golden corn pudding, sticky sweet potatoes, and the cloverleaf rolls that had been rising all morning. By the time the men came in, the house smelled like the finest restaurant in Indiana. I pulled the beaters out of the fluffy mashed potatoes, ran my finger along their sides, and tasted the warm, creamy goodness when Mom wasn't looking. Then I plopped a large pat of butter into the middle of the potatoes and watched it melt almost instantly until it looked like an enormous egg, sunny-side up.

"Mom, what do you want me to do now?" I asked as the

men reappeared, washed up and looking like they hadn't eaten in days.

"You can put the ice in the glasses. I'm going to ask your granddad to slice the roast, and then we'll eat."

It was Granddad's job to carve the roast, which he always did at the table with the expertise of a great chef.

The ice cubes clinked as I used the special silver tongs to drop them carefully in the crystal goblets to the right of each place setting.

"Don't forget ice for the grandchildren."

Frannie beamed a toothy smile.

"Frannie . . ."

I started to protest. Why waste ice cubes on glasses that no one would drink from? *Pick your battles, Lib.* That was what Mom always said, anyway. I decided a little frozen water wasn't worth a meltdown.

Frannie walked over to the little table and set down a name card that read EZMRDA EMLEE in green and red crayon.

"How many cubes would *Ezmrda Emlee* prefer?" I asked.

"Two, please. And three for Eugene. He likes his water very cold."

Clink. The grandchildren got their ice cubes.

At the table, we joined hands, and Dad thanked God for all the blessings our family enjoyed each day. With a hearty "Amen!" Ronnie was ready to dig in, but first, Granddad had to do his magic with the roast beef. And what a roast it was. While some families might slice up a holiday ham, we observed a long-standing tradition of enjoying the fruit of Ryansmeade, beef for Christmas dinner. Having slow-cooked all day, the juicy, rich brown meat now sat steaming

59

on Mom's enormous white platter with the holly berry design around the edges.

Granddad stood solemnly at the head of the table and clinked his knives together with great ceremony. Frannie giggled. By the time Granddad had the platter piled with moist slices of beef, we were all laughing. He took a bow, and Ronnie said, "Let's eat!"

The dinner conversation ranged from Purdue talk to Nowhere news and everything in between. Granddad and Dad were both proud Purdue grads, so between them there were a lot of Boilermaker stories to recall.

Frannie just kept asking, "What's a Boilermaker?"

Sometime after passing the sweet potatoes and the beef and noodles, Ronnie asked how my calves were doing.

"You can see for yourself after dinner," I told him.

"They eating well?" Ronnie asked, heaping more mashed potatoes onto his plate.

" 'Bout as good as you, Ronald," Granddad quipped, and everyone laughed.

"Yes, they are eating fine," Dad spoke up. "But I'd really like your opinion, Ronnie. Maybe we should adjust the feed some."

"Sure, I'll take a look."

I felt my face flush and I couldn't help but feel a little bit of resentment that Dad was still consulting Ronnie. These were *my* calves. This was *my* project. Why didn't he discuss feed with *me*?

"So, who's your biggest competition this year?" Ronnie asked. "The Evans kids got any good animals?"

Jack Evans's steer had won second place last year, taking home Reserve Champion. Jack would graduate from Nowhere High next June, and I knew he'd be trying harder than ever before for Grand.

"That Joseph boy has some mighty nice-looking cattle every year," Granddad offered, referring to Josh Joseph, a high schooler whose family raised Shorthorns.

"I don't know," I told him. "I haven't seen anyone else's calves yet."

"Those Darling girls seem to think they've got a chance this time around," Dad added. "Boy, wouldn't that make old Jim Darling proud?"

It'd make any dad proud. He didn't say it aloud, but I was sure that was what he was thinking. Suddenly, bringing home Grand Champion meant more than just honoring Ryansmeade. I wanted to make Dad proud, maybe even prouder of me than he'd ever been of Ronnie.

As far as the talk about the Darlings being competitive in the beef arena, the only competitions they had ever won were stupid beauty pageants. Still, I found even the possibility of Precious and her sisters winning the steer show quite unsettling.

The chatter continued through the pecan and sugar cream pies. Mom poured coffee into china cups with delicate handles and little saucers to match. Frannie and the grandchildren excused themselves from the table to play with Frannie's dollhouse.

Finally, Ronnie said, "Lib, what do you say we go out to the barn and take a look at those future champions?"

"Champion," Dad corrected. "Don't forget, Libby can only take one to the Practical County Fair."

I watched Dad try to place his great big thumb through the tiny handle on his coffee cup. He managed to get the dainty little cup to his mouth and then swallowed the coffee in one sip. He'd be glad to get his favorite John Deere mug back in the morning.

"Okay, *Champion*," Ronnie agreed, and we got our coats. Outside, the frosty air hit my face, a sharp contrast to the warm indoors. It felt good, refreshing. The day was turning to night, and it was going to be a clear one with stars by the millions dotting the black sky. Fourteen and a half miles from Nowhere, the stars had no lights to compete with. No streetlights, no traffic lights, no lights at all. It had snowed late last week, leaving a nice five-inch blanket of white on everything. The temperatures stayed below freezing, and for once we had known days ahead that we would have a white Christmas.

Our boots crunched in the snow-covered gravel as we crossed the barnyard to the barn. Piggy and Mule were comfortable in the straw, but even inside it was cold. I could see their breath appear in puffs of steam as they huffed and stood to greet us.

Piggy nearly bolted to the gate, snuffling around first in my palm and then in Ronnie's in search of a holiday treat.

"I don't have anything to give you," Ronnie told him. Unconvinced, Piggy kept butting Ronnie's arm to lift it so that he could continue to search Ronnie's pockets for something to eat.

Ronnie laughed.

"Is this guy always so hungry?"

"You bet he is. That's why I call him Piggy."

I got into the pen and had to use my shoulder to nudge the persistent Piggy away from Ronnie's empty hands.

"Do you really think it's a good idea to name your calves, Lib?"

Ronnie's face was serious. He sounded just like Dad. Immediately, I was defensive.

"Of course it's a good idea. Every calf needs a name."

"My fair animals never had names," Ronnie reminded me. He suddenly sounded so grown-up, so parental.

"Well, that's because you didn't get very attached to your fair calves," I told him, scratching Piggy just behind his left ear. As soon as I said it, I knew it was the wrong thing.

"Exactly my point, Libby. How are you going to part with calves you've grown to care about so much?"

I couldn't say I hadn't considered it, because the thought of letting go of Piggy had crossed my mind several times before. But I had been able to dismiss it with the knowledge that I had seen many a steer come and go from Ryansmeade. I had watched while Dad and Granddad loaded the livestock trailer with cattle to take to market. It hadn't particularly bothered me then, so why should it bother me now?

"It's no big deal, Ronnie."

I tried to sound convincing even as Piggy playfully wrapped his long, rough tongue around my hand, just as he had done in the pasture on the day I picked him out.

Mule, who had kept his distance and was standing in the

far corner of the pen, let out a long, low bellow as if to say I was wrong.

Ronnie and I both looked at Mule, who slowly turned his back to us. It seemed that was all anyone had to say about the subject of selling steers.

EIGHT

— learning to walk —

"What are your plans to control bovine spongiform encephalopathy?"

"What?"

"BSE."

"Huh?" I gave Carol Ann my speak-English-to-me-please look. It was a look I had perfected since becoming best friends with a brain.

"BSE. You know, mad cow disease," she whispered.

She stopped brushing Mule and stepped back as if just saying the words *mad* and *cow* aloud in the same sentence might contaminate the whole farm.

"It's an insidious disease, you know. It has the potential to bring down the entire American beef industry."

She was serious. Actually, serious was usually an understatement when describing Carol Ann.

"Get real," I told her. "That whole mad cow thing is really overblown."

"That's what you think, but one case of bovine spongiform encephalopathy here in Nowhere, and life as you know it would be over."

What a ray of sunshine Carol Ann turned out to be on that January day. Winter had arrived in Practical County with an arctic blast, bringing frequent snow showers that accumulated a couple of inches at a time, but not enough to do what all of us at Nowhere Middle School hoped: close school.

With winter darkness settling in by late afternoon, that left only Saturdays for spending time with the calves. And Carol Ann had spent several with me, in the toasty barn, brushing Mule and Piggy.

On this particular occasion, Carol Ann was wearing her favorite going-to-Ryansmeade bib overalls. Okay, they were her *only* pair of bib overalls. I continually told her she didn't have to wear them when she came to help me with the calves, because I knew very few farmers under the age of eighty who actually wore bib overalls. But Carol Ann wore them whenever she came so that she wouldn't look like a town kid, she said.

I wore my favorite barn clothes: holey blue jeans and a hideous pink sweatshirt with three goofy lambs embroidered on the front, a gift from my great-aunt in Ohio. It was a heavy one, so I wore it out to the barn often. And that way, when my great-aunt phoned to ask if I was wearing the shirt she made me, I could say, "All the time," and I wouldn't be lying.

"I'll ask Dad about bovine sponge-whatever whatever-whatever," I assured Carol Ann.

"Promise?"

"Of course I promise."

I certainly wouldn't want to be responsible for the fall of anyone's hamburger empire. Carol Ann must have decided that, at least for the moment, Ryansmeade was safe from devastating diseases, because she went back to work on Mule's tail with the metal comb. He never moved a muscle while she tugged the tangles out of the long, wavy hair.

Piggy, on the other hand, wiggled and stretched his neck, trying his best to reach what little corn might remain in the feed bunk. Finding nothing, he attempted to nibble on the brush I was using. That calf was always hungry!

It was amazing how the calves had grown. Dad said he thought Mule was well over four hundred pounds and Piggy at least five hundred. They'd lost their bony baby look and each one now stood strong and sturdy. There had been a time not too many years earlier when I would have been afraid of such a big animal. I remembered being Frannie's size and going out to see the cattle on pasture with Dad and Granddad. They seemed as big as elephants. But now, with the constant attention these steers were getting, I knew I was raising two gentle giants. By the time the fair came around next summer, each of them would tip the scales at more than thirteen hundred pounds.

"Ready to go?"

Dad came in with rope halters, one in each hand, a white cloud of breath hanging in the air in front of him. The thought of stepping out into the cold made me shiver. But it was a perfect winter Saturday; the sun on the snow, and the crisp, clean air made it as pretty a day as you can get in the middle of winter.

Dad started to put Mule's halter on, but I told him, "I'll do it."

He stopped.

"You know how?" He seemed surprised.

"Yes, Dad, I know how."

Mule stood motionless as I slid the halter over his fuzzy ears and tightened it around his wide black nose.

"Not bad." Dad nodded.

"Now Piggy's, please," I said, hand out for the second halter.

Piggy wiggled a little and twitched his furry head until I had the halter in place.

"Ready, Dad."

Dad pushed open the huge barn doors.

"Ready, Mr. Ryan," Carol Ann replied, her voice noticeably less convincing than her words.

I hoped she still wasn't thinking about mad cow disease. I soon found out it was cantankerous cattle, not contaminated hamburger on her mind.

"What if he jumps? Or runs? Or gets away from me?" She pounded me with questions as we headed out the double doors with the calves.

I laughed out loud.

"That's Mule you have there."

"So?"

"You'll see."

No sooner had the words left my mouth and Mule's feet hit the barnyard than the calf locked his legs. He nearly left skid marks in the snow-covered gravel.

Piggy and I continued forward, Piggy ambling alongside me with a steady, cooperative gait. What a good guy Piggy was. I beamed with pride at how he had learned so quickly to be led.

Behind me I could hear Carol Ann.

"Come on, Muley," she coaxed.

"It won't work," I called over my shoulder.

Carol Ann Cuthbert was not one to give up easily.

"Come on, little sweetheart."

She cooed in his ear while tugging gently on his halter.

"You gotta yank!" I yelled.

"I don't want to hurt him!"

I laughed.

"Do you want to move?"

"Yes! I'm freezing!"

"Then *pull*!"

She tucked her smooth brown hair behind her ears, a sign she meant business.

She pulled. Nothing happened.

Just then Dad came out of the barn.

"Here," he said. He reached for Mule's tail and brought it forward, pulling, but not too hard. Then he gave Mule a firm slap on the hind end.

Mule turned his head to see who had intervened on Carol Ann's behalf and took one reluctant step forward.

One. Carol Ann moaned, Dad chuckled, and I took Piggy once more around the barnyard while Carol Ann and Mule stood, going nowhere.

"Here, take Piggy," I ordered, handing Carol Ann his rope. She looked defeated.

"Tell me again why we're doing this," Carol Ann said, exasperated.

"Because," I explained, "fair calves have to be trained to walk and stand still on your command. The judge will never be able to get a good look at them if they don't stay still."

"Yeah, well, Mule over there seems to get the standing-still part just fine. But when it comes to walking, that animal is obstinate!"

She was right. Dad and I spent the next half hour push-ing and pulling an uncooperative Mule once around the barnyard. He planted his enormous hooves firmly in the snow when we tugged at his rope. I placed my back against his butt and pushed off the gate with my feet, and still, noth-ing. By the time we were done, we were exhausted, Mule was unhappy, and Carol Ann was feeling better.

"That is one stubborn calf," she remarked as we spread fresh straw in the pen to bed Mule and Piggy down for the night. Ten minutes later, with fresh water and a feed bunk full of ground corn in front of the calves, we headed for the house and two mugs of hot cocoa Mom had waiting.

Dad and Mom joined us in the kitchen just as winter darkness set in.

"How'd it go with the calves?" Mom asked as she set a plate of gingersnaps on the table.

I looked at Carol Ann and we both laughed.

"I have to admit," Dad told Mom, "these girls are pretty good calf handlers."

It was the first compliment related to the steers Dad had ever given me. I smiled at Carol Ann.

"You know," Dad said, "another month or so and you'll have to decide which calf goes to the fair this summer."

To me it was a no-brainer. There had never been a steer more perfect than Piggy. He was a good eater, gaining weight right on schedule. I had fallen in love with his sweet, cooperative nature, and I had already played the scene out in my mind. Piggy and me in the show arena, his black-and-white coat shining under the lights as I shook the judge's hand and accepted the blue ribbon. I just knew he would look and act great.

"Well, I know which one I'd take!" Carol Ann chimed in. She never was one to keep her opinion to herself.

"Don't be too quick to judge," Dad cautioned. "That Mule is one handsome calf. Straight back. Stands real nice on those front legs. It's too soon to know, but he may turn out more heavily muscled than Piggy."

What Dad said next fell on my ears like a giant thud.

"Yep, Mule might have the best shot at Champion."

I stared at Dad and for about half a second I considered what he was saying. Dad had seen enough steer shows to know what the judge would be looking for. And Dad seemed to see in Mule something that he didn't see in Piggy. It'd be unbelievable to come home with the top award my first year out. For one very short moment, I thought that Dad might have a point. Maybe Mule should be the one to go. Then I came back from fairy-tale land.

"Yeah, right," I said sarcastically. "The only way that stubborn calf will ever see the Practical County Fair is if he is served out of the Cattlemen's Club concession stand on a bun."

Everyone laughed.

But I meant it.

NINE

— jung chow's and
a really bad idea —

Friday-night pizza night was a tradition at our house. The best was cheeseburger pizza. Lots of hamburger, cheese, and onions piled on my favorite crust from Jung Chow's Pizza. Don't ask me how a pizza place in Nowhere got the name Jung Chow's. I guessed it was one of those little oddities that every small town has. Nowhere just happened to have a few more than most.

  Mom loved pizza night because she didn't have to cook. But she did have to drive. Jung Chow's didn't deliver, and even if they had, no one would have delivered fourteen and a half miles from town. The good thing was that when Mom picked up pizza, she picked up Carol Ann, too. So cheeseburger pizza night was also Carol Ann night at the Ryan's.

One Friday night early in March it was snowing like crazy when Mom was leaving to get the pizza. That was March in northern Indiana. Somewhere else it was almost spring. But in Practical County, it was snowing. Again.

"Coming?" she asked. The car keys were clamped between her teeth as she rummaged through her purse.

"Yeah," I said just as she held up pizza coupons and spit out the keys. We climbed into Dad's four-wheel-drive pickup, which Mom liked to drive when there was snow, and backed out of the garage.

The yard was dark except for the golden glow the light from the barn windows left on the snowy ground. Inside the barn, Dad was taking care of the nighttime chores with Frannie's assistance. She had given the barn cats winter names like Snowbell, Icy, and Blizzard. Never mind that they were all black and gray.

As we headed toward the lights of Nowhere, Mom filled me in on her latest listing. A doctor's house on North Oak Lane with four bathrooms and an inground swimming pool. She was really pumped up about this one because a house with a high price tag meant a high commission for Mom. I flipped through the radio stations looking for something I would like *and* Mom would tolerate while she went on about the hardwood floors and the chandelier in the entry.

"This just may be my biggest sale yet, Lib."

She sounded so excited. I knew each sale made her feel a little better about going to work. Mom hadn't always been a career woman. She stayed home and helped on the farm when Ronnie and I were young. But not long after Frannie was born, she got her real estate license. She loved her job, and she often mentioned how good it felt to be helping with the family finances. But she also felt guilty about having less time to spend with us and about leaving Frannie in day care. I honestly couldn't see why. Frannie was one of the brightest, happiest four-year-olds I knew.

"That sale will sure help the farm out this year," she added.

I felt a money talk coming and wished we lived seven and a half miles from Nowhere. Money was not a huge deal in the Ryan house. Mom and Dad both worked hard and we never wondered where our next meal would come from. We weren't rich, but we had all we needed and a little left for some of the things we wanted. But, like that of all farmers and cattle growers, Dad's income was unpredictable. Cattle prices went up and down, weather dictated what kind of crop year it would be. And now Ronnie was in college, and that was expensive.

"Kiddo," Mom started.

I hated being called that, but I guess there are worse pet names a parent can use.

"You know how it is. Even though we have several years to save for your education, we still have Frannie's college fund to think about."

We both laughed at the thought of Frannie in college. She'd run the place. I could just see it.

"*As president of the Student Senate, I, Frances Ryan, declare today and each day henceforth to be Macaroni and Cheese Day. . . .*"

"Every little bit helps," Mom continued. "Your savings

account will get a little boost this year with the sale of your fair steer. Ronnie was able to add something to his college savings each year he showed."

She was right. Every exhibitor sold their fair animal at the livestock auction, which meant receiving a nice premium over market price. That thought should have excited me, but for some reason, the idea of profiting from the sale of Piggy made me uncomfortable.

"And, you know, I was thinking . . ."

Uh-oh. Caution sign ahead. Not on the road. In the conversation.

"Why don't you participate in the Beef Princess pageant this year? The winners get savings bonds, you know, and think what a great experience it would be, and . . ."

Mom kept glancing from the snow-covered road to me to judge my reaction to her suggestion. I stared out the dark window so she couldn't see my face.

The Beef Princess pageant? She had to be joking. That was for chirpy girls like the Darlings.

As much as I wanted to avoid talking about money, I wanted even more to avoid anything that had to do with the Beef Princess pageant. There definitely could not be a reason good enough to get me up on a stage under a red striped tent on a sweltering July afternoon standing beside the Darling divas plus Ohma and answering questions like, "If you could create any dish in the world with a rolled rump roast, what would it be and why?"

"Libby, are you listening?"

Finally, I turned from the window to look at her. Now Mom would see my disbelief.

But she chose not to look. She kept her eyes on the road and continued to state her case.

"It would be such a fun girl thing for us. We just haven't done much together since you got your calves. Do you know how much fun it would be to try on dresses? We could go to Fort Wayne to shop, and . . ."

She didn't stop. She went on about Mrs. Somebody's daughter from work who could put my hair up in a French twist. Dresses? I hated dresses. Mom knew that. And what was a French twist anyway? It sounded like a doughnut.

Mom was sitting stiffly, grasping the steering wheel with both hands, and not looking anywhere but straight ahead. Was she being careful because of the snow, or was she avoiding the you've-got-to-be-kidding look on my face? She had to know it was there.

"Oh, look, we're at Carol Ann's house already!" she said cheerfully. "My, that was a quick trip."

At last she looked in my direction, smiling. If she could read my expression, she gave no indication whatsoever.

"Aren't you going to the door to get Carol Ann, kiddo?"

TEN

— the day that never should have happened —

It was a day I replayed in my mind a thousand times. It was a Saturday morning, and I had slept late. I never got chores done very early on Saturdays. The vet said a couple of hours probably wouldn't have made much difference anyway. But I wondered if she just said that to make me feel better.

Early spring in Indiana was the weirdest time of year. One day it was sunny and the daffodils were six inches out of the ground, and then the next day the wind was blowing and there was freezing rain falling, covering those daffodils with ice. You just never knew what you were going to wake up to.

On this particular Saturday, the rain hitting my bed-room window sounded more like sleet. And my bed, my warm, wonderful bed, felt so good. I knew Dad would call when he thought I'd slept long enough. So I stayed toasty and dreamy long after Frannie had popped out of her bed, gathered her grandchildren, and headed for the kitchen.

"Libby."

I opened my eyes slowly. It was Dad's voice. It didn't sound right. The clock read 10:28. By 9:00, Dad would usually be half disgusted that chores weren't done, but his voice was quiet. And close. He wasn't calling from the bottom of the stairs.

Turning, I saw him standing in the doorway, damp with rain and looking serious.

"Lib, you need to get dressed. The vet's on the way."

"The vet. . . ."

What? I wasn't awake yet. Maybe if I closed my eyes again Frannie would be standing there, rambling on with one of her stories. But as soon as they were closed, it was Dad who called again.

"Libby!"

The sharpness in his tone wasn't something I heard often. Suddenly, I was wide awake.

"Your calf is hurt. He got his leg caught between two metal gates—"

"In the barn?" I asked. I was out of bed now, digging through the clothes on my floor for a pair of jeans.

"No, in the feedlot. He spent the night outside lying on the ground with his front leg wedged between the gates. He fought to get loose, so he's cut up pretty bad."

It just figured that Mule would do something like that. Stubborn thing. I found jeans and grabbed a sweatshirt.

"I'm coming," I told Dad.

"I'll be outside." He turned and was halfway down the stairs when I asked:

"Is Mule going to be okay, Daddy?"

"We'll know more when the vet gets here. And it's not Mule, Lib. It's Piggy."

Did I hear him right? *Piggy* was the one who was hurt? Sweet, gentle Piggy?

"I think I hear the vet's truck. Meet us outside."

My fair calf. I hurried to dress and passed Mom in the hallway with the phone tucked between her shoulder and ear and a basket of folded laundry in her hands.

"Mom . . ."

I knew better than to interrupt her conversation. She gave me the not-now look followed by the I-know-all-about-it-and-it'll-be-okay look.

Ugh! Why couldn't my family communicate with real words like most others did? I flew through the kitchen where Frannie was standing before two rows of empty chairs with a Bible open in one hand.

"Shhh!" she warned sternly. "We're having church."

Ugh! Why couldn't my family communicate with real *people* like most others did?

I found Dad and Susan Hansen, one of three vets at the local practice, in the feedlot behind the barn. My heart sank when I saw that Piggy was down. Susan had put a blanket on him right where he lay as the rain-sleet mixture continued to fall.

"Can't he be inside?" I shivered.

At the sound of my voice, Piggy bent his head back to see me, his big black eyes wide and anxious-looking.

Susan stood up, wiping her wet hands on her dark blue coveralls. She was nearly as tall as Dad and thin as thin could be. She looked like she'd snap in two like a twig if she bent over the wrong way, but I'd seen her wrestle a steer into a treatment chute. And I had been there when Susan helped a cow drop twins right in Granddad's pasture. I was glad she was there that morning. I trusted her as much as anyone to help Piggy.

"Hello, Libby." She smiled, pushing a stray curl away from her face with the back of her hand. "Your dad tells me this guy might be headed to the county fair next summer."

I wanted to answer but couldn't, so I nodded. Piggy, who was usually so spirited, lay almost motionless. I knelt beside him, staring in disbelief as Susan's voice continued.

"He needs to stay put until he can get up on his own. He'll be warm enough under the blanket. And the temperature out here is rising, so I'd say he's been through the worst of it."

Through the worst of it. Her words echoed in my head. The worst of it had been in the night. For hours, Piggy lay outside, trying to free himself from the gate. And all morning, too. This freezing, miserable, wet morning while I was cozy in my bed, Piggy was out here. The tears wouldn't hold any longer.

Dad came over and squeezed my shoulder.

"Susan says he's going to be okay, Libby."

"Your dad's right. I don't think this leg is broken. There

may be some muscle damage to his shoulder. Time will tell. But that leg is banged up pretty good, and I could use some assistance cleaning it up. Want to help?"

Of course. Wasn't it the least I could do?

Susan opened her bag and began to clean and wrap Piggy's wounds. With trembling hands, I cut the gauze and tape and stroked his damp neck while she worked. His skin was usually so warm, but now his body temperature seemed dangerously low.

Inside the barn, Mule bellowed, unhappy about being separated and displeased that Dad had blocked the doorway out to the feedlot.

You be quiet, I thought. *You're the one who should be out here. You're the troublemaker, not Piggy.* Mule bellowed again.

"There we go. You'll be just fine." Susan patted Piggy and wrapped the remaining bandages into a ball.

Piggy let out a long, low, pathetic moo. He didn't sound fine, he didn't look fine, and I was sure he felt awful.

"Libby, I really mean it when I say that I think your calf is going to be okay. But he needs to get up on his own and I'd really like to see that happen in the next few hours. If it doesn't"—she shifted her gaze from me to Dad—"call me right away."

Dad walked with Susan around the barn to her truck. I sat with Piggy until Dad returned.

"I think he's looking better already," he said cheerfully, but it sounded forced to me.

"Dad?"

"What?"

"Do you think Piggy's going to get up soon?"

"You bet I do. It's downright nasty out here! Wouldn't you get up and go inside if you were Piggy?"

He chuckled, and I smiled. I knew how hard he was trying to make me feel better.

"Daddy?"

"Yes?"

"Do you think that Piggy will be able to walk the same after he gets up?" I dared to ask.

I knew Dad wouldn't lie to me. I also knew he knew what I was really asking.

"I don't know, Lib. I don't know if he'll be good enough to show after this. If he is crippled, he won't feed out well. We'll just have to wait and see." He drew a deep breath. "Right now, I need to rewire these two gates so that something like this can't happen again."

I turned back to Piggy. His mouth was opened slightly, his tongue lay loosely to the side. I was terrified he might die right then and there. I laid a shaking hand on his flank. It quivered at my touch, but then I felt the rise and fall of his breathing. It was fast, matching the pounding of my own heart. I smoothed his wet black hair, matted from his overnight struggle to free his leg.

I wanted him to be standing in the warm barn with me brushing his smooth, sleek body. Instead, he looked half frozen and totally exhausted. I promised I would stay with him until he got up, no matter how cold I got.

I owed him as much.

* * *

That night, Mom and I discussed Piggy's misfortune while we did the supper dishes. Granddad had eaten with us, as he did most nights.

"Not because I can't rustle up some good eating all by myself," he would say, his eyes twinkling. "But because better dinner companions can't be found this side of Nowhere."

I had hardly eaten, still devastated over Piggy's accident, and Granddad had tried to cheer me up with some ridiculous stories.

"I had a steer once that broke all four legs at the same time."

Dad groaned. He'd obviously heard this one before.

"Really?" a wide-eyed Frannie asked.

"You bet. Couldn't walk at all. Just sat there in the dirt in the middle of the pasture."

"Really?" Frannie repeated.

"Yep. Know what I called that steer?"

Granddad was asking me.

"No, Granddad," I said, humoring him. "What did you call him?"

"Ground beef," he roared. "Get it? *Ground* beef."

He slapped his knee, and I couldn't help but crack the smallest smile. Granddad was so ornery. I knew he would do anything to make me feel better.

Mom handed me a damp dinner plate and I rubbed the pear-green dish towel absentmindedly over it so many times that Mom finally took it out of my hands.

"I think it's dry now, Libby."

"Oh, Mom, I wish I hadn't slept so late this morning," I

cried. "If I had found Piggy earlier, maybe he wouldn't be so hurt now."

Piggy had gotten up on his own about an hour after Susan left the farm. He had hobbled into the barn and collapsed on the warm, dry straw. That was where he stayed, not willing to try again to stand up.

"It's okay, kiddo," Mom tried to tell me. "It wasn't your fault. Sometimes things just happen."

There really wasn't anything she could say that would make me feel any better. And I think Mom knew it, too, because she took the first opportunity she had to change the subject.

"Hey, how about you and I do a little shopping tomorrow after church?"

Shopping. Shopping was okay. I needed new work boots. Mine were getting kind of tight in the toes. And if I had a new pair of jeans for school, I could use one of my older ones for barn jeans. Maybe shopping would be fun.

"Okay." I shrugged.

"We could go to Warsaw . . ."

Warsaw? Why go all the way to Warsaw? I could get jeans and boots at the Wal-Mart in Nowhere.

Oh no.

". . . to that cute boutique where they sell fancy dresses and—"

"*No!*" I heard myself shout.

Mom looked surprised.

"Libby . . ."

How could she think that buying a silly dress for the stupid Beef Princess pageant would make me feel better?

"I'm not doing it, Mom. I'm not going to buy a dress, and I'm not going to be in that stupid, lame pageant."

I threw the dish towel on the kitchen counter and ran for the barn. Behind me I could hear Mom's voice, but I didn't slow down to listen.

The warmth of the barn was welcoming. In my rush to get away from Mom and her shopping suggestion, I hadn't even stopped to grab a coat. The freezing rain of morning had turned into plain rain, making everything feel and smell damp. I flipped on the lights, and three barn cats came running.

As expected, Mule was up and Piggy was down. I felt a little better when I saw that Piggy was sitting, his head high, and that the feed pan I'd placed in front of him was mostly empty.

Swinging my legs over the gate, I jumped into the pen and took out the feed pan.

"You doing better now, little guy?"

Piggy's shiny black head bounced up and down slowly a couple of times, as if he were nodding. It made me smile and feel good for the first time since I'd gotten out of bed that morning.

I stroked his sleek side, while Mule stood silently watching near the gate.

"You had a rough day there, fella. But you're going to be just fine. Aren't you, boy? You're going to be just fine."

Again his head moved up and down, slowly.

"Yes, you are. You have to be okay. I'll help you get better, okay, Pig?"

I got a rice brush from the nail on the wall and stroked him while I talked. Mule stepped a little closer, as if he might want to hear what I had to say, too.

"You don't know much about the Practical County Fair, but it's just the most magical, wonderful place there ever was. And this summer, I can take you there with me. And you can wear a fancy leather halter and walk around in front of the judge. It'll be so cool, Piggy, but you gotta be able to walk real good, see?"

Piggy didn't respond, but behind me, Mule mooed softly. I changed the subject.

"Do you want to hear about my mom's crazy idea?"

Piggy let out a deep, long breath.

"My mom thinks I should be in the Beef Princess pageant at the Practical County Fair. Now, isn't that the dumbest thing you've ever heard? Me? In a *pageant*?"

Piggy sat very still.

"Come on, Pig. You've been very agreeable so far. I mean, really. Think about it. The Darlings are the princesses of pot roast, not me."

I looked at Piggy.

"What do the Darlings really know about beef, anyway? I'll bet that they don't brush their calves every day. I am sure Precious can't tell a Shorthorn from a Hereford. And that Lil, she's so ditzy I bet she'd have to study her steer long and hard to figure out which end to put the halter on."

For the first time I wondered, *How is it that for four years Precious and Lil have been chosen as Practical County's spokespersons for the cattle industry?*

How much sense did that make?

"Piggy," I asked, "you don't think *I* should be in that stupid old Beef Princess pageant, do you?"

Without so much as a blink of his big black eyes, Piggy turned his nose to my cheek and nuzzled my ear. I wrapped my arms around his neck and squeezed.

"I knew you'd understand," I told him lovingly.

Beside us, Mule let out a loud bellow.

"Who asked you?" I grumbled. Then I put the brush away and turned out the lights.

ELEVEN

— thinking practically —

Some decisions in life are made with our hearts. Some are made with our heads. Sometimes, as I learned in early May of the year of Piggy and Mule, we make choices based not upon what we want, but what makes the most sense.

Susan had been out to the farm a half-dozen times to check on Piggy's progress. It had been a long, difficult month with Piggy hurt and Mule bellowing his fool head off in the next pen.

Piggy still wouldn't put his full weight on that right leg and he walked like a crippled old man.

"Give him a cane," Frannie suggested.

I wasn't in the mood for her antics.

"Frannie," I started, my patience just about gone, "do you know what you are? You're a—"

"Dorable?" she asked, head tipped to one side, eyelashes batting.

There was such a thing as too cute, and when Frannie crossed that line, it made me want to puke. Suddenly, I had an awful thought. No, more like a vision. I could picture Frannie growing up to be a Darling. All prissy and self-centered. She was well on her way. Oh no, I couldn't let that happen!

Note to self: Fix Frannie before it's too late.

But first, I needed to fix Piggy before it was too late.

Susan's truck pulled up the gravel lane just as the sun was setting. I loved how the days stretched out longer and longer in May until we slid into summer before we even realized the season had changed. This year, though, I wasn't anxious for summer to arrive. I needed to buy some time. Time for Piggy to heal.

Susan parked her truck in front of the barn.

"Hi, Libby. How's Piggy today?"

"He's doing great," I answered enthusiastically. I was really hoping she'd give me the go-ahead to take him to the fair in July.

Susan nodded but said nothing. Dad came out of the house and joined us at the gate beside Piggy's pen. I stroked Piggy's head.

"He's looking much better," Susan told us. "But he's really not using that leg like he should.

"Walk him once for me, would you, Libby?" she asked, her forehead wrinkled under her curly bangs.

90

I hopped into the pen, haltered Piggy, and then took him for a couple of rounds inside the fence. It wasn't easy for Piggy. He hobbled more than I thought he would.

Over at the gate, Dad and Susan spoke too quietly for me to hear.

"He'll make it, then?" I asked when I finally brought Piggy back, tying his lead rope to the fence.

"Well, yes, he'll make it, Libby. I never doubted that."

Susan sounded like she was choosing her words cautiously.

"About the fair, Libby," Dad started. "Piggy's not exactly a show calf in his condition, I'm afraid."

I stopped scratching Piggy's ears. He put his head under my arm and lifted it several times as if to coax me to continue.

"But I could still show him if I wanted to, right?"

I looked to Susan for confirmation. She looked at Dad. So did I. I already knew what was coming.

"Listen, Lib, all along I've been telling you that Mule's the better animal," he said.

"Better how?"

"Better all around. He's got a better frame. And he's filling out that frame just about as good as I've seen any calf fill out. And he's got a nice disposition."

"Dad!" I nearly sputtered. "He's stubborn! Remember, that's why we named him Mule!"

"Oh, he's as calm as they come. He just won't walk, but we can work with him on that."

"Okay then, he's *lazy*!"

Dad laughed. I didn't see anything funny about the conversation.

91

Susan smiled.

"Think of it this way, Libby," she said. "At least you didn't lose Piggy on that morning in March. He's a great steer, he made it most of the way to market weight."

What was she saying?

"Chances are," Susan continued, "he won't gain much more anyway, because he likely won't eat well in his condition."

That was crazy. Piggy always ate well. He was Piggy, after all. But since his accident he had gone off feed twice for a day or two. He really hadn't gained any weight.

I turned to Dad for support.

"Dad . . ."

"Libby, Susan and I agree that the best thing to do is to sell Piggy now. I don't want to take a chance on that leg getting any worse. You know that stockyards only take animals that can walk in on foot. We need to cut our losses and sell him right away."

Dad sounded so matter-of-fact, I couldn't believe what I was hearing. It was like he was making a business decision, not talking about my sweet Piggy.

Sell Piggy *now*? I felt the tears burn my eyes at the thought. Before the fair? Before he got a shot at Grand Champion? That was so wrong.

"No, Dad! We can't *sell* him." The sound of my trembling voice only made matters worse.

I couldn't fall apart in front of Susan. I didn't want her to see me bawling like a baby. I bit my lip hard to keep it together, but my stomach was in knots.

"He's big enough already that he's going to make great

freezer beef," Susan said, as if that somehow made it all okay. "Every market animal gets sold eventually, right?"

I didn't know what to say. Of course, she was right. I'd known since I was a little girl that the animals in our pasture would end up in someone's freezer, on someone's table. But somehow I'd made it so much more. All these months, I had made it about Piggy, my companion, my . . . pet.

"That's right," Dad agreed, a certain finality in his voice.

He brushed his hands off on the front of his coat.

"Raising good-quality beef is what this farm is all about."

It was lunchtime the following day at school before I could fill Carol Ann in on Susan's latest report and Dad's completely insensitive decision to sell Piggy. We carried our trays to an empty table in the corner of the noisy cafeteria and sat down.

"It just came from out of the blue, Carol Ann," I said, venting. "My dad just up and decided that a crippled calf isn't worth feeding any longer."

Carol Ann opened her milk carton, but not before turning it over to check the expiration date.

"You know, Libby, raising beef isn't my forte, but it seems to me that the reason you feed a calf is to make him bigger, right?"

I nodded.

"And bigger is better for turning that steer into a great steak, right?"

Carol Ann had such a way of making everything so black-and-white.

"To a point," I explained. "You don't want a steer to get too fat."

"Okay, so bigger is good, but too big is bad."

I nodded again, not sure where Carol Ann was headed with this. She pulled a pencil from her binder and started scratching numbers on her napkin.

"Okay, so how much do you think Piggy weighs now?" she asked.

"Maybe nine hundred and fifty pounds," I guessed.

"So if today's cattle market is three dollars a pound, then he's worth about two thousand eight hundred and fifty dollars, right?"

That sounded about right.

"Okay, so say he's not eating well," she continued. "He doesn't gain any more weight, and instead starts to lose a few pounds a week."

I was starting to figure where Carol Ann was headed, and I didn't like it much.

"So, see, Libby, your dad's decision makes the most sense. It's called cutting your losses, quitting while you're ahead."

Carol Ann was seeing this whole situation from a business perspective, just like Dad. I glanced down at my lunch tray. A lukewarm hamburger and soggy fries stared up at me. Why do people eat this stuff?

Carol Ann knew how much Piggy meant to me, so why was she taking Dad's side? Just as I was about to tell her she was being an insensitive brainiac, she came through for me.

"Of course," she said, "that's looking at it from the

practical side. And you know, the farmers in this county invented *practical*."

She laughed at her own play on words, then got serious.

"But, wow, Lib. Selling Piggy? Now, before you even get to show him, is awful. I'm so sorry."

Carol Ann's brown eyes were filled with concern, and she looked as though if I cried, she'd break down and bawl great big old tears of sympathy right alongside me.

"I just can't believe Dad was so cold about the whole thing. I think both of my parents are going nuts, Carol Ann."

"Your mom, too? What's up with her?"

I had never mentioned the Beef Princess pageant to Carol Ann. I knew she'd despise the idea.

I looked around to be sure no one could hear me. Between the clatter of silverware against trays and the roar of a hundred middle school students talking, I was sure I was safe.

"She wants me to enter this year's Beef Princess pageant," I said in a low voice. "Isn't that the most ridiculous thing you've ever heard?"

I knew Carol Ann would be all over this one. I was certain she would tear apart the whole idea in a heartbeat, which was why I nearly fell off my chair when I heard her say, "That's perfect!"

"What?"

"Oh, Libby, this is just too great."

She was on the edge of her seat now, her untouched tray pushed to the center of the table.

"You know, don't you, what a travesty it is that those atrocious Darling sisters keep winning that pageant? And, yes, it is a pageant, but there is so much more to it than a beauty contest."

"But—" I started to protest. Too late. There was no stopping the wheels in Carol Ann's mind once they were in motion. And now they were turning full speed ahead.

"Somebody has to stop them, Lib. Think of it, you could be the hero that saved Practical County's beef industry."

That was a little over-the-top even for Carol Ann. But her thoughts were not far from those I'd had brushing Piggy in the barn the night I'd snapped at Mom.

"I don't know, Carol Ann."

"Listen to me," she said in her most logical voice. "The Darlings have managed to make a mockery out of this pageant for four years running. They shouldn't represent the beef industry. They can't raise beef, they can't talk intelligently about beef, and they are lousy showmen. Am I right?"

"You are right!" I declared. Her impassioned pleas were starting to work.

"So you'll do it?" she asked with a hopeful expression.

"Maybe. I guess I could."

My ears could hardly believe what my own mouth was saying.

"Yes! You'll be awesome, Libby! I know it!"

"You know what, Carol Ann?"

"What?"

"You should go into politics."

"Oh, no, I don't think so," she replied. "I'm too smart for that!"

I took another look at the no-longer-warm hamburger on my tray. It didn't look very appetizing. It made me think of the Cattlemen's burgers at the fair: hot, thick, and juicy. So good that a slice of cheese was all a person needed to plop on top. No need to smother a Cattlemen's Club hamburger in ketchup. Just thinking about it made my mouth water. In a few short months, I could have all the Cattlemen's burgers I could eat. I was just about to force myself to take a bite of my less than appealing cafeteria burger when the bell rang, signaling the end of our lunch period.

"Thank goodness!" I declared, standing with my tray. Behind me, my chair hit something with a loud thud.

I turned to see the back of my chair smack-dab against the back of a chair from the table behind me. And who had just stood and pushed that chair back? None other than Ohma Darling herself. We just stood there, looking first at the collided chairs and then at each other.

Had she heard the conversation between Carol Ann and me? My brain did a quick rewind and replayed what was said. I was reasonably sure we hadn't said anything like, "Ohma Darling is the grouchiest, oddest, and most un-queenlike person to ever enter the Practical County Beef Princess pageant."

Well, at least we hadn't said anything like that out loud. But we had talked about how very wrong it was to allow the Darlings to represent the cattle growers of Practical County.

I made a quick decision to act like she had heard nothing.

"Hi, Ohma." I smiled.

"Move," Ohma growled.

Well, so much for hearing nothing.

I stepped aside, even though Ohma was far less threatening than her vicious older sisters.

Carol Ann saw an opportunity to confront Ohma and grabbed it.

"What were you doing spying on us in the ladies' room at the soup kitchen? And don't deny it. We know you were in there!"

Ohma was silent for a moment, and then she opened her mouth to speak. I waited to hear what she would say when she didn't have her sisters around to imitate.

"I didn't . . . I . . . my sister . . . I wasn't . . . ," she stammered, as a look of distress spread across her round, red face. Finally, she just let out a loud "UGH!" and ran from the cafeteria.

Carol Ann and I had no idea what to think.

"That is the most unusual human being I have ever met," Carol Ann declared.

We dumped our trays and headed to class before the next bell.

At home that night, I decided to tell Mom that I'd made a decision. I was setting the table and she was draining the pasta for supper.

"I've been thinking about the Beef Princess pageant."

Mom's head snapped up, her eyeglasses steamy from the boiling pasta water.

"You have?" she asked, putting the pot on the stovetop. She walked over to me, wiping her glasses with her shirttail.

"Yeah, well, I guess, if you want me to . . ."

A huge smile spread across Mom's face, and I hadn't even finished yet.

"I could maybe enter the pageant this year."

Mom was all over me in a heartbeat, hugging me and grinning ear to ear. I knew she'd be happy, but she was *ecstatic*.

"Oh, Libby! This will be so much fun! We'll go shopping and we can take Carol Ann along, too, if you'd like. You won't regret it."

She nearly danced around the kitchen as she put dinner on the table. I was glad that I could make her that happy just by agreeing to do something she suggested. Seeing Mom so thrilled was reason enough to have changed my mind. But the real reason was the one that had come to me in the barn, the one that Carol Ann had confirmed earlier that day. And that was to make sure another year didn't go by with a Darling sister representing the beef growers of Practical County.

That, however, meant that I not only had to *enter* the Beef Princess pageant, I had to *win* it.

TWELVE

— this little piggy
went to market —

On the final Saturday in May, Dad drained the last of the coffee from his John Deere mug and announced, "It's time, Libby. I'm taking Piggy in today."

In. I knew what *in* meant. In to town. In to McClure's Slaughterhouse.

It had been two weeks since Dad had decided that Piggy would be sold, so I wasn't surprised by the news. But I wasn't ready, either.

"You coming along?"

I pushed the eggs around on my plate with the back of my fork. I certainly wasn't going along.

"No."

"Libby, you really should come with me. You need to, you know, see this project through to the end."

I raised my eyes to figure out if this last statement was a suggestion or an order. Dad had a determined look on his face. A that's-the-way-it's-going-to-be look.

I'd been to McClure's many times. When I was little, it was such a treat to ride along when Dad and Granddad took a load of steers. While the men unloaded out back, Ronnie and I would run into the front store and Mrs. McClure would hand us each a stick of spicy, chewy beef jerky. It would last all the way home.

Even the fond memories of McClure's couldn't convince me to jump in Dad's truck that day and lead Piggy to slaughter.

I messed with my eggs a minute longer.

"Well, if you're not going along, you can at least go get his halter on him," Dad instructed. "I'll pull the truck and trailer up to the barn."

I couldn't believe he was being so mean. I didn't want to go to the barn, I didn't want to see Piggy, and I didn't want to say goodbye.

He took his hat from the rack beside the door and was almost gone when I stopped him to ask the question I'd been dreading asking for the last two weeks.

"Dad?"

"Yes?"

"Is Piggy going to end up . . . I mean, are we going to . . ."

I didn't want to say it out loud.

"Eat the meat ourselves?" Dad finished for me.

That was what I hadn't wanted to ask.

"No, Lib," he said. "I sold half to a neighbor and the other half to Mom's boss, Roger. Our freezer's plenty full as it is. Okay?"

"Okay," I said, and out the door he went.

It was a relief knowing that Piggy was going someplace other than our table. Eating our own beef was nothing new to me. It was just that our other steers never had personalities. I'd never gotten to know them before. And I'd never given them names.

Careful there, Dad had said months ago. *Fair calves don't need names*.

"Are you all right, Libby?" Mom asked, pulling out a chair at the breakfast table.

I pushed my plate away. I was done playing with my eggs.

"This isn't the way this was supposed to happen, Mom. Piggy should have gone to the fair."

"Things don't always work out the way we plan, Lib."

What a typical mother answer.

"I just didn't think I'd get so attached to my steers."

"Well, that's to be expected when you spend as much time with any animal as you've spent with Piggy and Mule."

"They are so wonderful, Mom," I tried to explain. "They have personality. Piggy is sweet and Mule is stubborn, but they're both so gentle."

"I know, kiddo. I am sure it is really hard to say goodbye."

Goodbye. I had to go say goodbye. I slipped into my boots by the back door and went slowly out to the barn. Piggy was lying down in the straw. Mule stood near the door that led to the outside lot. When he saw me, Piggy got up. He came right over, his crooked gait more obvious than ever.

I was already crying. There was nothing I could say to him to make this moment feel any different. Piggy nuzzled my hand for food and I felt his rough, wet tongue lick my palm.

I could hear the pickup truck pulling up to the barn, and I knew Dad was waiting. Piggy's red rope halter slipped effortlessly over his ears, he didn't even twitch them. I opened the gate and led him out of his pen.

Dad appeared in the doorway, his square jaw set.

"Ready?"

"No."

"It's time to go."

I buried my face in Piggy's velvety neck as the tears poured from my eyes.

"Goodbye, Pig" was all I could manage to choke out.

Dad took the lead rope from my shaking hands and led Piggy into the stock trailer, latching the gate behind him.

"Sure you don't want to go along?" he asked once more.

I couldn't speak. I shook my head and turned back to the barn. The sound of the pickup grew fainter as it traveled down the gravel lane to the road, but I didn't turn around to see it go.

Back inside the barn, Mule bawled once, loudly, and paced slowly from one end of the pen to the other. I put my head down on the feed bunk, wondering if the tears would ever stop. If saying goodbye to my steers was going to be this hard, maybe Dad was right. Maybe showing steers wasn't for me after all.

Just then I felt a familiar nudge, a wet leathery nose that, for a split second, made me wonder if Piggy was still there. I lifted my head to find Mule softly nuzzling my tear-soaked face. I had never noticed how very blue his eyes were. He moaned quietly, and I realized that he, too, would have to adjust to life without Piggy.

THIRTEEN

— feathers and fluffy stuff —

The very next day, Mom, Carol Ann, and I were shopping at the mall in Warsaw. Mom was convinced a girls' day out was just what I needed to chase away the Piggy blues. Trouble was, the reason for the trip was enough to send me back into the depths of self-pity all over again. We were on a mission, out to find a dress suitable for a pageant that I wasn't too sure I wanted to be part of in the first place.

It really was a stretch to call the shopping center a mall. With barely a dozen stores, it was nothing like what they had in Fort Wayne or Indianapolis. But even Warsaw had more to offer than Nowhere.

We were in Betty's Boutique (the name alone should have been warning enough) and I was in the dressing room with several potential pageant dresses hanging around me. I looked in the mirror at what I had worn from home. Jeans, a plain blue T-shirt, and flip-flops.

Nothing wrong with that, I thought.

But Mom and Carol Ann were camped out just outside the dressing room door, waiting for me to appear wearing something fancier than my everyday clothes.

"Try the teal one on first, Libby," Mom hollered loud enough for the entire boutique to hear.

"I'm right here, Mom," I grumbled through the cardboard-thin door that was open at the top and bottom. "You don't need to yell."

I wasn't sure, but I thought I heard Carol Ann snicker.

Okay, let's get this over with.

I took the teal dress from its hanger and held it up in front me while I looked in the mirror. Ugh. It had puffy sleeves and tons of fluff around the skirt. I pulled it over my head and opened the door, looking around to see if anyone else was in the boutique besides Mom, Carol Ann, and Betty, the somewhat robust shop owner who made it her business to tell customers exactly what she thought they wanted to hear.

"Oh, *darling*, you look simply adorable," Betty cooed, adjusting the glasses she had just snatched from the chain around her neck.

I really wished she hadn't said "darling."

I had taken one small step outside of the dressing room when she grabbed my elbow and pulled me in front of three mirrors. The outer two were tilted inward to catch the reflection from the one in between.

Oh, great, now I get to see my hideous self in multiples of three.

Mom agreed with Betty. Carol Ann just sort of scrunched up her nose and lips and gave me a subtle head shake. I didn't need to be told more than once. I ducked back into the dressing room and shed the teal fluff as fast as I could.

The next one was pink. It had a little pink around the neckline and a pink overlay on the skirt. It also had a light pink sash and dark pink sleeves. And did I mention it was *pink*?

Again, I ventured out of the dressing room to be met with applause from the adults and a look of horror from Carol Ann.

"That one is just *precious*, dear!" Betty exclaimed. Once again, a poor choice of adjectives.

I took a long look in the three-way mirror and had to bite my lip to keep from laughing. I was certain I had seen the ruffly, pink image in the mirror before. In a cartoon, maybe. Flying, dipping in and out of chimneys, waving a magic wand and spreading magic dust all over the Land of La-Di-Dah. I looked like a fairy.

"Try the yellow one," Carol Ann suggested, and I shot her a glare. The yellow one had feathers on it. It screamed Big Bird to me.

She shrugged as if to tell me there wasn't much she could do about my unfortunate situation. It went on like that for almost an hour. Too short. Too long. Too Cinderellaish. Too ugly stepsisterish. One wispy ruffled dress after another until the dressing room was so piled with pastel tulle it looked like a clown had melted on the floor.

When I eventually emerged from the dressing room in my own comfy jeans, Mom was just breaking the news to Betty that we hadn't found what we were looking for.

That was a relief. Mom wasn't going to insist that we "make something work," as she so often did when we shopped.

"Thank you so much," Mom politely told Betty, who seemed a little rattled that we hadn't fallen in love with a single dress she had to offer, and we ducked out of the boutique without a dress.

On the front porch that evening, while Mom read a real estate magazine and Dad held an issue of *Beef Producer* on his chest as he snored in his rocker, I sat watching Frannie chase lightning bugs around the yard. The ones that didn't escape her grasp were stuffed into a mayonnaise jar with holes punched in the lid. She was making her own nightlight before bedtime.

Although it wasn't unusual to spend summer evenings on the front porch, there was a reason why no one was inside tonight. Mom's eyes frequently left her magazine to check the road from the west. Ronnie's truck would pull in any minute from West Lafayette, and he'd be home from college for the whole summer.

Waiting never was one of my strengths. I came down from the porch and slipped away while Frannie plucked more bugs from the air. I didn't really want her to go to the barn with me. I hadn't ventured in there since Dad had taken Piggy, and I was curious to see how Mule was doing.

"That animal's been crying his fool head off," Dad had

told me when we arrived home from our unsuccessful shopping trip.

It was no surprise to me. Mule hadn't been without Piggy since they were both just days old, and I felt more than a tiny bit sorry for him.

The tall, heavy sliding door was already open to let in the coolness of the early-summer evening. Mule was standing in the pen, looking very alone and making sure the whole farm could hear his complaint.

"Mmmmmmmmmmmmmmm." It was a sad, low noise.

"I know, Mule. I miss Piggy, too."

The straw in the corner where Piggy liked to lie was still matted down. Mule paced anxiously around the pen. It was the most I'd ever seen him move.

He looked nice, clean and smooth, long and lean. I had been so consumed with Piggy's accident, I hadn't noticed how much Mule had filled out. He looked straight and strong. He even seemed a little more willing to cooperate with me when I talked to him. Had I misjudged him all this time? Or had I just favored Piggy so much that I'd failed to see Mule for what he was?

His muscular sides twitched to shake off an occasional horsefly. I grabbed a can of fly spray and joined him in his pen. He stood still while I sprayed him down.

"There, that should keep you more comfortable."

"How about a little walk around the barnyard?" I asked as I slid the halter over his big, fuzzy ears. They twitched back and forth. I clipped the lead rope onto the halter and opened the gate.

"Come on, big guy," I coaxed, and to my amazement he

walked right away. Maybe he was losing some of that stubborn streak.

Smoothly, he strode around the barnyard, his huge hooves crunching in the gravel. I pulled him from the front, tugging now and then to keep him going.

"That's the way, Mule," I praised him. He was a beautiful animal, pitch-black and velvety, with those gorgeous blue eyes. Why had it taken me so long to notice those wonderful eyes?

"Looks like you got him trained."

The familiar voice came from behind me.

"Ronnie!"

"Hey, Lib. I just pulled in and saw the lights in the barn."

"Look at how good Mule is walking tonight."

Ronnie walked over and patted Mule's side.

"I was just noticing that. I can see you've been working with them."

I winced when he said *them*. He must have noticed.

"I heard about Piggy being sold."

"It wasn't fair, Ronnie," I started to protest.

"Now, listen, Lib. A crippled steer isn't a profitable investment."

I should have known I was wasting my breath. He and Dad were just too alike.

"I know. I heard it all from Dad."

Ronnie was kind enough to let it go.

"Well, I see Mule's learned a lot since I was last home. But it looks like *you* could use some work."

Me? What was wrong with me?

"Take him around again, and let me see what you're doing."

I frowned. I wasn't sure I wanted to be judged by my big brother.

"Go on. I'll give you some pointers."

I tugged on Mule's lead rope to get him moving again. He hesitated a few seconds but then got going. We made a quick circle and stopped in front of Ronnie.

"There," I said. "No problems."

"Well, no, if you're taking your steer for a walk," Ronnie explained. "But you're not. You're *showing* the animal, Libby. Here, let me have him."

I handed the rope to Ronnie.

"You be the judge," he said.

"Well, I think I like this better." I smiled.

"What I mean is, you stand in the center of what we'll pretend is the show arena. Right here."

He made a mark in the gravel with the toe of his boot.

"The judge is going to be in the center while the animals are walking."

"I know that, Ronnie. Are you forgetting that I've watched you show steers since I was Frannie's age?"

"I know you know, but have you ever looked at the show from the judge's perspective?"

He had a point. I'd never thought of that.

I stood in the middle of our make-believe arena while Ronnie walked Mule around me several times.

"Notice where I am," Ronnie called from behind Mule.

"I can't see you very well," I answered.

"Bingo!" Ronnie replied. "That's just what you want. It's not *you* that the judge needs to see. It's the animal. So you want to keep the animal between you and the judge at all times."

That made sense. I was sure no one had ever explained that to the Darlings. Whenever they were in the arena, they were trying to be the center of attention.

"Now," Ronnie continued, "I'm taller than you are, so I can see over Mule's head. That's important because I need to keep my eye on the judge at all times. Let's switch places."

I took hold of Mule's rope and Ronnie once again became the judge.

"Oh no! I can't see you over Mule's head."

"That's what I thought. Just take a step backward, keep ahold of the rope close to the halter, and straighten your arm."

I did as Ronnie said and it worked. Now that I had backed away a little, I could see Ronnie's face right over Mule's shoulder.

"Okay, go around again."

I tugged to get Mule going, but he wouldn't move. I tugged again. Nothing.

He was up to his old tricks. I let out a long, exasperated sigh and pulled harder.

"Wait," said Ronnie, stepping out of his judge's role to help me. "First of all, never let your frustration show. As a showman you must remain calm and in control at all times." He smiled and added, "Even if you're not."

Then he took the rope from my hands and said, "Try this."

Ronnie held the rope firmly at the halter and pulled quickly on it, then let go. Mule felt the pull forward, and expecting it to continue, he pulled back to resist. When Ronnie didn't continue to pull, Mule stopped resisting. One more short tug and release and Mule stepped forward.

It was amazing.

"What a cool trick!" I exclaimed as Ronnie and Mule started around the invisible arena. "What else can you show me?"

Ronnie laughed.

"I'll give you some pointers on how to set him up and then we'll call it a night."

Ronnie showed me how to use the long silver show stick to place Mule's feet in perfect position. It was important to keep him set up before the judge, he explained.

"Go ahead, now," said Ronnie. "You set him up."

I took a long look at Mule's hooves. His right leg was too far forward, so I took the show stick and poked it gently into the crevice in his hoof. He lifted that leg and set it right back down in the same spot.

I did the same thing again. And so did Mule. One more time with the stick, and Mule placed his hoof right where it had been before.

Okay, if I couldn't move his right leg back, I'd move his left leg forward. I felt like an absolute genius for thinking of that. Carol Ann would have been proud.

I used the stick, which had a tiny hook that wrapped around Mule's hoof, to pull forward just a bit on his left leg. Like magic he responded, taking one small step with his left foot.

A quick check of his front legs, his beautiful straight back, and I knew I had it.

"There. Done!" I declared triumphantly to Ronnie. No sooner had the words left my lips than Mule shifted his weight, wiggled backward a step or two, and took one big step forward, leaving all four legs out of position. I was right back where I started from.

Ronnie had made it look so easy. But when I tried, Mule didn't cooperate at all. I tried again and again, but every time I got him set up perfectly, he stepped out of it, and I had to start all over from the beginning.

Finally, exhausted and frustrated, I pulled Mule over to Ronnie and surrendered.

"I give up," I announced. "I am supposed to do all this *and* keep my eyes on the judge? You've got to be kidding!"

Ronnie patted my shoulder as he led Mule to drink before putting him away for the night. "You're doing just fine, Libby. We've got plenty of time this summer to refine your technique."

I wished I had half the confidence Ronnie had.

FOURTEEN

— the clock started ticking —

When school let out, the countdown began.

Six more weeks until the Practical County Fair. Five more weeks until the Practical County Fair. Most years I counted the days with excitement, anticipating the most celebrated week of the year. I looked forward to running around the midway with Carol Ann, bumping into class-mates I hadn't seen all summer, chewing on gooey caramel apples, and, of course, devouring the tastiest burgers ever made by the Cattlemen's Association.

This summer, the huge feeling of anticipation was still there, but I found that when my thoughts turned to the Practical County Fair, a certain, well, uncertainty made my stomach flip-flop just a little. The carefree days of being the little sister were behind me. I had the responsibility of showing Mule. And I had the Beef Princess pageant staring me in the face. Even the thought of a juicy Cattlemen's burger was less appetizing than it had been in the past.

Ronnie and I took Mule out to the feedlot daily to practice walking and setting up his feet so that he would stand just right for the judge. By the end of the month, I was feeling more confident in Mule's ability to behave himself at the fair.

"It looks like you're my only shot at Grand Champion, Mule," I told him after a fine practice session. For the first time, I was convinced of something Dad and Granddad had known for a long time: Mule was indeed a Grand Champion contender.

If only I had been able to find that same sense of confidence about the Beef Princess pageant. Things in that department were not going well at all. Ohma had definitely overheard the part of the conversation between Carol Ann and me when I said I'd enter the pageant, and she had no doubt told her sisters, who were taking advantage of every opportunity to point out that the title of Practical County Beef Princess had remained in the Darling family for years.

The Darling sisters were easy enough to ignore once school was out, but in a town the size of Nowhere, you run into folks everywhere. And the canned-goods aisle at the IGA is no exception.

That was where I was on a Friday evening in June, when I ran into Lil and Ohma. Mom and Frannie were on the other side of the store, and I was searching for a can of marinated artichokes. The two younger Darling sisters were fighting with each other. I heard them before they even came into view.

"Shut up, Lil. You don't know what you're talking about."

That was Ohma, for sure. I would have known that low, grumbling voice anywhere.

"Oh, please. You are just jealous that I can wear the dress and your pinky toe won't even fit in it."

Ouch. That was severe, even for Lil.

"Oh, yeah, well, I wouldn't wear that stupid dress if I had to. It's ugly."

Just then they rounded the corner. Lil had on a short flowered skirt, a hot-pink tank top, and flip-flops with a giant daisy on her big toe. She looked fairly together, but she'd been taught well by her older sister. Ohma, who could never seem to pull off the same look as the other Darlings, was wearing a pair of neon yellow shorts and an old T-shirt. Her hair was in her face, which was red from yelling at Lil. Seeing me, they quickly stopped arguing. Lil flashed her famous smile. Ohma kept the trademark scowl.

"Well, it's Libby Ryan!"

"Hey, Lil. Hey, Ohma."

"I heard a rumor that you're going to enter the Beef Princess pageant at the fair this year."

"Yes, I am," I said, holding my head high.

"You realize, don't you, that this is a *beauty* pageant?" Lil questioned, her painted eyebrows arched high. She looked me up and down, and for a moment I wanted to disappear into the shelving. But I stood tall and shot right back at her.

"Actually, it's a contest to find the best spokesperson for Practical County cattle producers. You should know that."

I was feeling pretty good about my comeback. Then Ohma blurted out a bald-faced lie.

"Libby has been telling everyone she can beat you, Lil. I heard her say it."

"Ohma, that's not true," I defended myself.

Lil laughed coolly.

"Maybe you could beat me. In your *dreams*!"

Stick to the facts, Lib.

"Oh, it's no big deal, really. I'm just entering for the fun of it."

I tried to sound casual, and I wondered if I was pulling it off. I'd nearly choked on the word *fun*.

"No big deal?" Lil squealed loudly. "Yeah, right, Libby. The Beef Princess pageant is, like, the highlight of the Practical County Fair!"

"Well, I'll see you there, then." I smiled and ducked into the next aisle.

I found a can of marinated artichokes for Mom and met up with her and Frannie near the checkout.

As we loaded the back of the van with sacks of groceries, I thought about the encounter with Lil and Ohma. Lil certainly had the beauty-queen image, just like Precious. I was sure she had the wardrobe for it, too. And me, I had jeans, a ponytail, and no dress.

It's really no big deal, I told myself. *No big deal.*

FIFTEEN

— a girl thing —

With the fair growing ever closer, I began dwelling more and more on the fate of Mule. He had actually won me over, and I found that I was enjoying working with him.

One warm summer night, after bedding down his pen with fresh straw, I watched him kick and run around. He wasn't a calf anymore. He had hit the thousand-pound mark a while ago, but watching him play in the fresh straw like a puppy made me laugh.

Mule dug his nose deep into the slick, golden straw and lifted his head high, making straw fall everywhere. He kicked it around with his hooves and jumped forward. Then he ran from one side of the pen to the other, almost sliding into the barn wall as he came to a halt. His cheerful enthusiasm reminded me of Piggy. I missed him dreadfully.

Mule skidded up to the gate, panting from his romp in the straw.

"Come on, Muley," I said, grabbing his halter. "I've got a real treat for you!"

I led him out into the lot and tied him to the fence. Summertime heat in Indiana could be brutal, and we were on our sixth day of highs in the nineties. The heat was bad enough, but the humidity was even worse. Humans could escape to the air-conditioning, but animals had to find other ways to cool off.

Pulling the hose into the lot, I turned on a gentle stream of water and let it run down Mule's back. He lifted his head high and twisted it as far as the rope would allow him so that he could see what was going on.

"How is that?" I asked, as his hooves danced in apparent delight. I let the water run over his neck and under his chin, the only place on his muscular body that was fleshy and floppy. He stuck out his huge tongue to lick the water from the hose.

"I'll be right back. Stay put," I instructed, and then laughed at my own words. Of course he was going to stay put. One, he was tied, and two, he was Mule.

I returned from the barn with a bottle of show soap, poured some in my hands, and then rubbed it into one of Mule's massive sides. He stood still, loving every minute of it. The lather turned him instantly from black to bubbly white as I washed away the barn smell, bits of straw, and dried manure. I soaped up his tail until it was so slippery I could no longer keep ahold of it when he swished it to one side or the other.

As I rinsed the suds from his glistening body, his sloppy, soppy tail swung around and smacked me squarely on the shoulder.

"Hey, you," I called. "Quit that."

I moved to the other side. *Whack*. His tail came around to that side and hit me.

"Mule!" I laughed.

He was doing it on purpose. Time and time again, his tail found my arm, my shoulder, even my face. He was enjoying this little game, and I couldn't stop laughing.

Mule gave me the most innocent blue-eyed stare when it was all over and I led him back to his pen.

"Mule, you're quite the steer," I told him.

In a few short weeks, the pen would be empty, and Mule would be gone, too. First the show, then the auction. That was the way it would go. I really hated to think about it, but I couldn't avoid the truth.

In bed that night, as I tried to picture myself leading Mule around the auction ring, the tears came easily. With Frannie snoring softly in her own bed, I cried for the first time since I'd said goodbye to Piggy. The tears flowed at the thought of having to part with yet another steer. Then I heard the hardwood hall floor squeak, and I flipped over, quickly pretending to be asleep. Too late. Dad had come into the room.

"You still awake?"

"Yeah."

"What are you doing up so late?" he asked.

"Nothing. Just thinking."

Dad sat down on the end of my bed.

"What's on your mind, Libby?" he asked.

"Dad, why can't we just keep him?" I blurted out. It wasn't the way I would have wanted to bring up the subject, but I didn't have much time to organize my thoughts.

"Your steer? Libby, you know that you have to take your fair project to auction, and—"

"But I would feed him, I promise, and he is so tame, he wouldn't get wild, even if he gets really, really huge."

Dad just sat there.

"Please, Daddy, we can just keep him in the barn. I don't want to sell him."

"Listen, Lib, cattle are raised to produce food," he said. "Steers are not pets. They need to be sold at market weight. Otherwise, their meat will be no good, and all the feeding and caring you've done for them will be for nothing."

Fine, I thought. *Let all the other steers sustain the world. Let Mule sustain me!* I felt like my heart would stop beating if I had to part with another animal.

Dad stood up and patted my head like I was a little girl. He handed me the tissue box from the dresser top and stood at the door for just a moment.

"Libby," he said seriously. "I was afraid of this from the very start. Maybe this whole cattle-showing business isn't for you."

"What do you mean?" I asked, blowing my nose.

"Maybe it's just not a girl thing," he said into the darkness.

I couldn't believe he was bringing up the whole "girl thing" again.

"Dad!" I was raising my voice.

"Shhh, Lib. Frannie's sleeping. What do you say we move this conversation downstairs?"

I slid out of bed and together we went down to the kitchen, where Dad poured two glasses of cold milk.

We sat at the table, and I started again.

"Dad, haven't I shown you that I can take care of my animals just as good as Ronnie did? Haven't I fed and cleaned and trained Mule?"

Dad nodded. "Yes, Libby, you have done a fine job. Better than I ever imagined a girl your age—"

I groaned when he said "girl."

"Okay," he corrected himself, "better than I ever imagined a *person* your age could."

I was pleased with his admission. He hadn't thought I could raise steers, and I had proven to him that I could.

"But, Libby, the toughest part is yet to come."

I knew what he meant.

"You've already been through it once. You know what it feels like to let go. That's why I made you go out that morning and halter up Piggy."

I felt guilty, remembering that I had thought he was being mean. He was just making me face what would happen at the end of every steer project. They all end with goodbye.

"Daddy," I admitted, "I don't know if I can do it again."

"Tell you what, Libby," he said, placing his hand over mine. "You have to do it one more time, at the fair, with

Mule. And then if you decide showing cattle isn't for you, you won't have to do it again."

It was kind of him to say, but the truth was, I *wanted* to show steers. I wanted to be part of the Ryan family tradition. And I wanted more than anything to be strong enough to let go of Mule.

"I can do it, Dad. I know I can."

SIXTEEN

— independence day —

It was the Fourth of July, a holiday the Ryan family always did in a big way. As a result, the wheat harvest and straw baling were put on hold, Mom shut off her cell phone, and Ryansmeade was transformed into picnic paradise. The front porch became a smorgasbord of potato salads and baked beans, fruit dishes and desserts. Table after table of summer recipes lined the porch railing. Mom had invited the usual assortment of friends and neighbors. Carol Ann and her family were there. With the hardware store closed for the holiday, the Cuthberts hadn't missed a July Fourth celebration with my family since Carol Ann and I became best friends. Frannie was thrilled to have all of Carol Ann's younger brothers and sisters to play with.

Granddad was in charge of the grill and everything that went on it. Standing there in his stars-and-stripes apron, he'd wave his hamburger spatula and grin at everyone who drove up the lane. Nearly every guest commented on the wonderful aroma coming from the grill. The smell of summer, the smell of the Fourth of July, America's hamburger holiday.

From the porch, it was just a few steps down to the most wonderful outdoor dining room you could imagine. Picnic tables sporting red, white, and blue tablecloths took center stage under the enormous oak. Frannie was placed in charge of dozens of tiny U.S. flags on sticks, which she very randomly stuck around the garden, in flower pots, and in her hair. All afternoon she had been bouncing around in a headband that sported red and blue glittery stars on springs, so every move of her head was a patriotic event.

Granddad flipped a hot, juicy burger onto Ronnie's plate. Ronnie lifted it to his face and inhaled deeply.

"Ah! Burgers on the grill! Beats dorm food any day."

After having Ronnie home for several weeks, it was almost like he had never left for college. Dad was in a great mood with Ronnie around. Mom just kept hugging him and accusing him of growing taller. Frannie even gave Ronnie one of her grandchildren to look after while he was home.

"You better take Eugene," she explained. "Esmerelda Emily wouldn't be interested in doing the boy things you and Daddy do all day."

Ronnie played along as he always did with Frannie's charades.

"I'll need another of these burgers, Granddad," he said as he smothered the one on his plate with ketchup.

"Already? You haven't had the first bite of that one."

"Sure I have," Ronnie said through a mouthful of burger. "Besides, it's not for me. It's for Eugene."

He winked at Frannie, who wore an ear-to-ear grin.

Despite the festive atmosphere, I just couldn't quite get myself into the mood to celebrate. I'd spent a lot of time thinking about Mule in the past few days. Every moment I spent with him made me appreciate him even more. Every time he blinked his long black lashes over those big blue eyes, I became more and more attached. The thought of selling Mule at auction so that he could be steak on someone's table became unbearable. I had promised Dad I could handle saying goodbye, and now I had no idea how I'd live up to that promise.

Somewhere between the potato salad and the mixed fruit on that Fourth of July fourteen and a half miles from Nowhere, another thought had occurred to me. Another way to defend my love for Mule. And if I couldn't free my steer from a horrible fate, I would at least take a stand on his behalf. Although I was completely unprepared, I was about to make an announcement.

I guess if I had it to do all over again, I would reconsider making that particular announcement in such a public manner at such a gathering as my family's Fourth of July party.

It didn't go over real well.

"Where's your burger?" Ronnie asked innocently when Carol Ann and I sat down at a picnic table next to him and two of his college buddies who were visiting for the holiday.

I glanced down at my meatless plate.

"In memory of Piggy, and out of respect for Mule, I hereby declare myself a vegetarian," I announced confidently.

Ronnie looked at me like I had two heads.

"Oh, really?" he challenged me. "Since when?"

"Since now, I guess," I replied, my confidence quickly slipping away. I should have known Ronnie wouldn't let this go without questioning it.

"A vet-in-arian!" Frannie cried. I hadn't realized she was around. There was no turning back now.

"Not *veterinarian*, Frannie," I started to explain. "*Vegetarian*."

"Mom!" Frannie screamed across the lawn. Mom was just coming out of the front door with another pitcher of lemonade. "Libby is a vegetable-arian."

Mom laughed. Others stopped talking and turned our way.

"It's *vegetarian*, dear," Mom said to Frannie.

To me she said, "Are you, kiddo?"

All eyes were on me. Dad stopped in his tracks with the tray of burgers he was carrying from the grill. Forks were poised in midair as people stopped eating to await my reply. I swear the birds stopped singing.

Had Libby Ryan, daughter of a cattle grower, granddaughter of one of Practical County's most respected cattlemen, just said that she would no longer eat meat?

"Well, I—I . . . ," I stammered. I hated being in the spotlight. "I, um, I just thought that, maybe, um—"

"She's taking a stand for the animals she loves dearly."

It was Carol Ann. Dear, clear-headed, articulate Carol Ann who spoke for me.

Friends and neighbors turned back to their plates and the buzz of chatter continued, only now I was sure it was about me.

"That's just weird, Libby," Ronnie said, shaking his head with an I'm-disappointed-in-you look on his face.

"Why?" I asked. "Why is it weird?"

"Because raising beef for our table is a part of our livelihood. It's what *we* do, Libby."

Part of me was surprised to hear Ronnie say "we" when he talked about the farm. Any other time I would have thought that "we" referred to him and Dad and Granddad, the men, the farmers. But the way he said it told me he meant to include me. I had somehow earned a place in the "we" that was Ryansmeade. It didn't matter to Ronnie that I was only twelve and a girl.

Truthfully, I didn't know what to say. He was right; raising cattle was our family's work, our tradition. But I was right, too, wasn't I? I had the right to stand up for my steers, didn't I?

Mom and Dad both came over to the table to join us. Dad's forehead was wrinkled with concern.

"What's all this about you being a vegetarian, Libby?"

"What about chicken?" Mom asked. "Is this strictly a beef boycott or are you really going to be a vegetarian?"

Dad looked at her like she was nuts.

I didn't have all the answers to their questions. I hadn't

129

given much thought to this whole vegetarian thing yet. Surely I wasn't the first person in Practical County to become a vegetarian. Somewhere in Nowhere there had to be at least one other vegetarian. I just couldn't think of one.

Chicken, turkey, ham? I wasn't attached to any chickens, turkeys, or pigs—not like I had become attached to Piggy and Mule—but I didn't want to appear wishy-washy on the subject.

"Nope," I said firmly. "No meat. It's just disrespectful to our fine furry and feathered friends. Besides, is it fair that we Americans get to pig out like this when there are people starving all over the world?"

I knew that would strike a chord with Mom, the food-pantry champion of Practical County. Dad gave Mom a look-what-you-started stare.

That night in the barn, while I fed Mule, Carol Ann and I discussed my announcement.

"Whoa, Lib, that was some bomb you dropped!" Carol Ann sounded both proud and surprised.

"I had to do *something*," I told her as I scattered a leaf of fresh green hay into the feed bunk. "Mule's going to die, Carol Ann. Do you realize that?"

"Sure I do. That's been the plan all along, right?"

"Well, yes, but it seems so unfair. I can't keep him forever, and I don't see any particularly brilliant spiders in this barn weaving webs with complimentary messages over Mule's head, do you?"

Carol Ann laughed.

"No, I don't."

Then, as if vegetarianism weren't already confusing enough, Carol Ann had to complicate the issue even more.

"So, what kind of vegetarian are you going to be, Libby?"

"What kind? I didn't know there were different kinds."

"Of course there are."

I had to have a walking search engine for a best friend.

"Are you a vegan?" she inquired.

"Am I a what?"

"A vegan. They not only reject meat, they don't eat other animal products either. You know, like eggs and milk."

"I don't think Mom would be too happy if I stopped drinking milk."

"Oh, okay, then you are probably a lacto-vegetarian. Unless you're going to eat eggs, in which case you are a lacto-ovo vegetarian."

For crying out loud, I hadn't expected this whole vegetarian thing to become so complicated. Still, I wanted to do it for Mule's and Piggy's sakes.

"Okay, whatever, Carol Ann. I guess I'm that last one. I mean, it doesn't kill a chicken to lay an egg, does it?"

Barn chores done, I switched off the light for the night and we headed back to the house, where old Grove Everett was preparing for his annual fireworks show. The sun had set on a gorgeous summer night, warm and clear. Carol Ann and I gathered Frannie and the littlest Cuthberts on a big blanket to watch the starry sky fill with colorful bursts of blue, red, green, and yellow. We oohed and ahhed for an hour.

Well past midnight, sleepy children headed home with their parents, and all our guests were gone.

"Leave that for morning," Mom insisted when Dad and Ronnie started folding up lawn chairs and wiping off tables.

I climbed into bed and listened to Frannie's quiet snoring and the dull thud of far-off Fourth of July celebrations that continued into the night.

· What a strange day it had been. I was proud of the stand I had taken for Mule and Piggy, but I had a feeling that it wasn't enough. Tears brought on by confusion and frustration fell to my pillow as I drifted off to sleep. I couldn't shake the nagging feeling that I could do more to help Mule.

I don't know what woke me later that night. The popping of firecrackers had subsided, and the house and world outside it seemed still. Frannie slept motionless in her bed across the room and even the crickets were silent. My tears were gone, but the ache remained when I thought of Mule asleep in the barn.

All of the emotion that had built up over the spring and summer felt fresh and new, and my head was spinning. I had a desperate need to do something, anything, to stop the inevitable. The sense of urgency was too much. Not even sure of what I was doing, I got out of bed, dressed quietly, and tiptoed down the creaky old farmhouse stairs. I'd never noticed in the daytime how incredibly noisy they were. The kitchen was dark, my parents' bedroom door shut. From a hook in the garage, I grabbed Ronnie's flannel shirt.

It wasn't until I had slipped out the back door and into the summer night that I knew exactly what I was going to do on that Independence Day.

SEVENTEEN

— avocado and alfalfa sprouts —

The sun streamed into my bedroom window and fell across my face. It was hot for morning sun, the promise of another scorcher. My first thought was of Mule. I'd have to be sure he had plenty of water.

Mule. Oh, wait. Mule. Had I dreamed it? Or had I actually done it?

I sat upright, trying to make sense of the events of the night before. I remembered leaving the house. The full moon had illuminated the barnyard so much that I hadn't even needed a flashlight as I made my way to the barn.

The sliding doors had been open as usual on warm summer nights, so the animals hadn't noticed my presence until I spoke.

Mule had been sitting close to the gate. The barn cats scattered, and overhead in the mow, something had skittered, a raccoon perhaps. Mule had lumbered to his feet when I'd opened his pen and stepped inside. He ambled over to me as if to ask what I was doing there in the middle of the night.

I remembered talking to him, stroking his smooth black head, and leading him into the back lot. I remembered that I hadn't even cried when I told him goodbye.

And then, I opened the gate and watched him walk out into the night.

Oh, my gosh! I *had* done it. I had set Mule free.

What was I thinking?

Now very awake and nearly panicked, I jumped from my bed, grabbing shorts to pull on with the T-shirt I was already wearing. I tripped down the steps, my mind racing wildly. Why had I done that? It seemed so right at the time. I had reasoned that between Dad, Granddad, Ronnie, and me, we'd never really know who "accidentally" left the gate unlatched, we'd chalk it up to being one of those things that happens, and Mule would be spared a tragic fate and . . .

And what? He'd roam around Practical County being fed by strangers like a stray pup?

Oh, this was the stupidest thing I'd ever done. Cattle occasionally had gotten loose around here, and nothing good ever came of it. I'd heard the stories, at the dinner table, sitting at the counter at Cuthbert's Hardware. I'd heard about cattle loose for so long they turned wild, couldn't be caught, and had to be shot before they hurt someone. I'd heard about one of Mr. Erickson's steers that ran out in front of the mailman's car. Totaled the car, killed the steer. The mailman was lucky; it could have been far worse for him.

Now, thanks to my own middle-of-the-night madness, Mule was out there, wandering the flat farmland of Practical County. How far could he go in—I looked at the clock as I stumbled through the kitchen—eight and a half hours! Forget Practical County—he could be halfway to Indianapolis by now.

I paused long enough in the kitchen to read the note on the table.

LIB,

    RAN TO TOWN FOR GROCERIES. TOOK FRANNIE. DO YOUR BARN CHORES.
LOVE, MOM

She obviously hadn't noticed that my steer was gone, or she would have woken me up. Not surprising, though, because Mom never did pay a whole lot of attention to what was going on in the barn.

I flew through the garage, pulling on rubber boots as I ran. Where was Dad? Granddad? Or Ronnie? They were probably getting the combine and wagons ready to cut wheat today.

But hadn't Dad gone into the barn this morning?

Outside, I scanned the horizon for a large, dark lump wandering through the fields. The corn was shoulder-high; Mule could be forever lost wandering around in a cornfield. The soybean fields were shorter, but the neighboring farmers would be hopping mad if a steer trampled their beans. My best hope of finding him would be in the fields of freshly cut wheat. His big, black body would stand out clearly against the golden straw.

The barn never seemed so far from the house. I flew through the sliding doors, praying for a miracle. And what I saw next darn near qualified as one.

I sank to my knees in the straw on the floor and moaned out loud in utter relief. Mule was standing in his pen, gate latched, noisily chewing his morning grain. I got to my feet, tears stinging my eyes. Inside the pen, I threw both arms around Mule's soft neck, felt his breath on my skin, and cried.

"I'm so sorry, Mule. I won't ever let you go again."

I brushed him while he finished eating, not wanting to leave his side. Had it all been a dream? No, I was sure it hadn't. But how, then, was Mule here now?

The proof that I hadn't been dreaming lay before me when I turned to go back to the house. Ronnie's flannel shirt, the same one I had grabbed in the night, was sitting on a bag of feed.

I carried the shirt to the house, hung it on the hook in the garage, and went into the kitchen. Pouring a glass of orange juice, I sat down at the dining room table and stared out the window at the tall green corn in the field and felt incredibly lucky that my steer was safe.

I still couldn't believe my lack of judgment the night before. If I really had let Mule loose, and there was no doubt I had, then who put him back in? I was sure it was only a matter of time until Dad came home and I would find out.

* * *

137

Mom was the first to return home that day. When I heard her call to me to help unload the groceries from the van, I tried to act like nothing had happened. She didn't show any sign of knowing about Mule's midnight adventure, so I didn't mention it.

With all the grocery bags in the kitchen, I started to put things into cupboards. Frannie handed me cans of tuna and boxes of macaroni. It looked like we'd be having tuna noodle casserole this week. I wondered if tuna was considered meat. Then Frannie started passing me things I'd never seen before. Avocado spread. Bean sprouts. Rice cakes.

"It's almost lunchtime," said Mom. "Why don't you girls leave out the sliced turkey, the deli roast beef, and the Swiss cheese, and, oh, yes, leave the avocado spread and sprouts for Libby to make a sandwich."

I was afraid that was what Mom had in mind when she bought those things.

Soon we had a tray of sandwiches ready for Dad, Ronnie, and Granddad. Among all those roast beef and Swiss cheese sandwiches, among the buns piled high with turkey, one avocado and alfalfa sprout sandwich stuck out. I was both surprised and happy that Mom was supporting my decision to eat differently than the rest of the family. I just wished I was as enthusiastic about alfalfa sprouts as she appeared to be.

EIGHTEEN

— granddad's secret —

The rest of July went so fast, I can hardly remember it. Most days were the same: I got up and fed Mule early so that he could be finished eating before his bath. I had started rinsing him daily so that come fair time, his hair would be clean and easy to groom. A cold rinsing on a hot summer day was good for hair growth. And I had learned from Ronnie that a thick coat of hair can make a decent steer look like a champion.

I had managed to stick to my word so far about being a vegetarian. I took to ordering my Jung Chow cheeseburger pizza minus the burger. I had been eating eggs by the dozen. Scrambled, over easy, hard-boiled, you name it.

Dinnertime had become particularly stressful. I would sit down, absolutely ravenous, and say, "Pass the . . ."

I would look around the table.

*Meat loaf, no. Fried chicken, no. Beef and noodles, no.
Peas, okay.*

"Peas, please."

Dad just shook his head each time I passed the pork platter without taking even a bite and asked for more broccoli.
To be honest, it was getting harder and harder to pass the
platter. The smell of the rich, warm meat would reach my
nose and my mouth would start watering. I was making myself miserable. But it was for a good cause, I told myself.
Mule was a good cause.

Granddad had remained strangely silent on the subject
of my new eating habits. I noticed he had been paying very
close attention to the conversation that took place on the
Fourth of July, but he had never mentioned it to me.

One hot afternoon when I had just finished washing
Mule, Granddad came out to the barn with a plate of watermelon.

"Why don't you join me for a little snack over here,
Libby?"

I worked the handle on the pump a few times until fresh,
clean water poured out. I washed my hands and joined
Granddad in the shade of the maple beside the granary.

"What's all this talk I hear about you lately?" he asked,
handing me a thick, cold slice of melon.

I'd known that Granddad would confront me about my
vegetarianism sooner or later. I figured that because he'd
been a cattleman his whole life, he'd have a pretty hard time
understanding.

Granddad's eyes were as blue as Mule's. I noticed that for the first time sitting there under the maple.

"Oh, it's nothing."

"Doesn't sound like nothing to me."

"I just decided that I would stop eating meat."

Keep it simple, stick to the facts. I would follow the advice he himself had given me.

"All right." He nodded slowly.

All right. Well, maybe Granddad was more open-minded than I thought he'd be.

"It's okay, Libby. You have every right to choose how and what you will eat. You're becoming a young lady with ideas of your own, and I'm proud of you for that."

His eyes twinkled the way they did back at the pasture the day he picked Mule out for me.

"I just want you to be sure that you are doing what you're doing for the right reasons. Seems to me you've been making some rash decisions without thinking things through first."

Rash decisions? Maybe I had kind of jumped into this vegetarian thing without researching it much, but . . . oh, Granddad's eyes gave away his secret, just as my guilty face must have given away mine.

"I think someone ought to check the latch on that steer pen. I found Mule outside the gate the other morning," he told me.

I should have known that a steer as tame as Mule wouldn't go far from his feed and the ones who fed him.

"You know anything about that?" Granddad prodded.

I nodded. I knew it was a stupid thing to do, but admitting it to Granddad was embarrassing.

"Granddad, I don't know why I did that. I was desperate. I just don't want to sell Mule at the fair auction."

"Okay." He nodded. "Let's say you don't."

"Okay. I don't." I could go along with that.

"So, then what?" he asked.

"What do you mean?"

"You show your steer, he does well or maybe he doesn't do so great, and then you don't sell him at auction. What do you do then?"

I was no dummy. Dad had already been through this with me.

"I know I can't keep him, Granddad."

"Okay, so what happens to him? If you bring him home, he's already market weight. If you keep him, he'll become overweight and not nearly as good as if you sold him at the right time. If you sell him from home, you've given up quite a premium at the auction."

"That's part of it, Granddad. I know some girls who show steers just for the money at the auction. I feel so guilty profiting from Mule's death."

Granddad was a softy. Maybe he would see my side of things when it came to parting with my steer.

"Libby, let me tell you something. Many years ago, when my parents came to this country from Ireland, they brought with them a knowledge of cattle and how to raise them. But even more than that, they brought with them a value of hard work and self-sufficiency. Do you know what I mean by that?"

I nodded.

"It's like this. Ryansmeade was built on tradition. We Ryans love this land, and we love the animals we raise on it. That's why they are so well cared for here. This year, you've had your first taste of raising cattle, and I can tell it's in your blood."

I knew what he meant. Whether I was in the pasture with the herd, or in the barn with my fair calves, I loved being with the steers.

"No matter what we choose to do in life, Libby, we learn to take the bad with the good. Letting go is one of the hard parts, but it's not just a part of raising cattle, it's a part of life, too."

I swallowed hard, fighting back tears that came at the thought of ever letting go of Granddad.

"This legacy is yours, Libby." Granddad's eyes scanned the flat farmland that stretched far beyond our house and barn. He gazed over it, silent for a minute, then turned his thin, wrinkled face to mine.

"You're old enough to know that there are folks out there who don't agree with our lifestyle. They think raising any animal for the purpose of eating it is wrong, and I understand that it's their right to believe what they believe. But I couldn't be prouder of my heritage, Lib. This"—he gestured around us—"this is what I know, this is what I believe in."

His blue eyes were filled with tears that didn't fall. I'd never heard Granddad speak so passionately about anything before. Mostly he and I talked about rain and how many kittens were born in the barn that week.

143

Granddad took a worn red bandana handkerchief from his pocket and dabbed his watery eyes.

"You'll know, dear. Maybe not today or even this year, but someday you'll know if you want to take part in the tradition of Ryansmeade. Just know two things. First, you are a Ryan and you will always be loved regardless of what you eat or where you choose to live. And, second, the Ryan family tradition is nothing to be ashamed of."

I didn't have any words to follow what Granddad had shared with me, but he didn't seem to expect me to say anything. A long, comfortable quiet passed before he spoke again.

"Now, try this."

He placed a watermelon seed between his front top and bottom teeth, drew in his breath, and spit the seed as hard as he could over the fence and into Mule's pen.

I laughed hysterically.

"I want to do it!"

I inhaled deeply and sent a seed flying just two feet in front of me.

"You can do better than that," he teased.

We practiced until there were no more seeds to spit.

I needed time to make sense of everything Granddad had just said, but it was okay. His words would echo in my mind for the next several weeks.

NINETEEN

— another man's treasure —

"I'm going to town, Libby!" Mom hollered from the house. "Want to come along?"

I quickly finished organizing the halters and ropes in the fair show box and ran to meet Mom and Frannie as the van was heading out the lane.

With just a few days until the fair, there were some things I knew we needed for Mule. Fly spray, for one. Nothing is more annoying to a steer than a horsefly on his butt.

"I need to go to the bank and the bakery . . ." Mom was listing all of her stops aloud as she drove toward Nowhere.

"Can we stop at the Feed and Seed, Mom?"

"Sure, that's fine. It's just down from the thrift store, and I have a bag of Frannie's clothes to donate."

In the backseat, Frannie was pulling articles of clothing out of a paper grocery bag.

"Hey, I can still wear this!" she cried, holding up a pink ballerina costume that had been too small since she was two years old.

"Frannie! Don't!"

"I'll get it, Mom," I offered, reaching into the backseat. I put everything back into the bag except the ballerina dress, which Frannie clutched with both hands.

"I have an idea," Mom said as she pulled into a parking spot in front of the bank. "I'll go to the bank and the bakery, if you don't mind running this bag into the thrift shop. Then you can get your fly spray at the Feed and Seed."

She handed me a twenty-dollar bill and the bag of clothing, and I headed toward Another Man's Treasure.

"Well, hello, Libby!" Mrs. Nipper nearly shouted when she saw me.

"Hi, Mrs. Nipper. My mom has some things for you."

"Oooo, goody!"

Mrs. Nipper took the bag from me and eagerly began to pull things from it, making over everything as if it were brand-new.

"Oh, Libby, your mother always gives me the sweetest things!"

Mrs. Nipper had a way of seeing treasure in everything.

"This is absolutely precious!"

She pulled the pink ballerina costume from the bag. How had Mom managed to get that back in there?

"Oh, dear, well, look at me. Here I am ignoring you, Libby."

She pushed the bag and its contents aside on the counter-top. I knew just what was coming.

"What is it *you* are looking for today, dear? I have some new jeans, just your size!"

By "new" she meant "just came in." Nothing in Another Man's Treasure was really new.

"Thanks, but there isn't anything I need. Really."

"Oh? Well, how about purses? You girls are always carrying the cutest little bags around. Come over here, dear, and let me show you."

I started to protest, but she had already come from behind the counter to take me over to where she had dozens of handbags displayed. Most of them looked like ones that had belonged to my grandmother, ones that Mom used to let me play with when I was little. I remembered filling them with Ronnie's Hot Wheels.

"Oh, thanks, but I have lots of purses."

That was a lie. But it was told with good intentions. I really needed to get out of there. I turned toward the door, and that was when I saw it. It was hanging on a hanger just inside the door. I must have walked right by it when I came in.

Mrs. Nipper never missed a sign that someone might be interested in something.

"Do you like that, dear? Well, it looks like your size. I just got it in. Cute as a button, isn't it? And a steal at four-teen ninety-nine, don't you think?"

She took the dress from where it hung and held it up to me.

"Take it in the dressing room. Go on now."

147

She nearly pushed me behind the curtain. The dress was so simple and pretty. A plain, light blue sleeveless dress. No ruffles, no lace, no *feathers*! Oh, it would be a miracle if it fit. Slowly, I put it on. So far, so good. I reached for the side zipper and pulled it up with ease. It fit!

I turned toward the mirror and took a long look. Unlike Frannie, who would wear a church dress to the barn if she were allowed, I had fought anything but blue jeans since I was a toddler. But this simple pale blue dress was like nothing I'd ever worn before. I stared at my reflection and actually liked what I saw. The sleeveless top showed off my arms and shoulders, which glowed with a midsummer tan. And the skirt shimmered just a tiny bit as it flowed gracefully to the floor, where it fell with a couple of inches of extra material.

Mom could take it up, I thought. But then I had another idea. I stood on my toes until the hem just brushed the floor. I would wear heels. *Nothing fancy*, I told myself, but my mind pictured something silvery with just the tiniest bit of glitter, maybe.

Everything was perfect. I played with my mousy brown hair. Even it didn't look so dull against that fabulous dress.

"Libby? Are you all right in there, dear?"

"Yes, Mrs. Nipper," I answered. "I'll be right out."

I took one last look at the perfect dress and quickly changed.

"I'll take it," I told Mrs. Nipper when I came out of the dressing room. I gave her the twenty-dollar bill. She handed me the change, put the dress into a bag, and talked me to the door.

"Libby, dear, do tell your mother I said hello and tell her

she can drop off anything anytime. Take care, dear, and stop back in when you need a new purse. . . ."

I could still hear her talking when I got out onto the sidewalk. I had solved the pageant dress dilemma all on my own, and I was feeling pretty good about it.

Now to the Feed and Seed. I prayed that fly spray was less than five dollars.

I turned to my left and found myself face to face with Precious, Lil, and Ohma Darling.

"What do we have here?" Precious sang. "Libby Ryan, coming out of the thrift store?"

"Yeah," Lil chimed in. "I bet she buys *all* her clothes there."

"I bet she buys all of *our* old clothes there," Precious said with a laugh.

Suddenly a terrible thought occurred to me. What if the dress, the perfect dress, had once belonged to the Darlings? My panic was brief, however, as I realized that it was likely far too ordinary a dress for them to have ever worn.

"Actually, I was just taking in some things my mom wanted to donate. . . ."

Why was I making excuses? What business was it of theirs if I *did* buy everything I owned there?

"Well then," said Precious, making a move toward me. "What's in the bag, Libby?"

I quickly shoved the bag behind my back. The last thing I needed was the Darlings picking apart the dress I had chosen for the pageant. Precious's grab for the bag missed, much to my relief, but Lil's reach was right on. She snatched the bag.

"Here, catch," Lil shrieked, and threw it high in the air, right over Ohma's head. It landed on the sidewalk behind her.

Ohma turned and lumbered toward the bag, but I was quicker, diving belly first on the cement for it before Ohma could get there.

I sat on the sidewalk, bag in hand and blood running down my knees.

"You idiot!" Precious and Lil screamed in unison. I looked up to see it wasn't me but their sister Ohma they were yelling at.

"Shut up," Ohma grumbled.

I stood, ready for the confrontation to be over, but Precious was just gearing up for another round.

"You ready for the fair, Libby? How did your *pathetic* little calves turn out?"

"Wait, Precious," Lil piped up. "Didn't we hear that one of Libby's calves didn't even make it?"

The mention of Piggy infuriated me. Was nothing private? Even in a place like Nowhere, you would expect that some things could be kept out of the rumor mill.

"Yeah, that's right." Precious nodded. "I heard she *poisoned* it with bad feed."

Well, it seemed the rumor mill wasn't always accurate. I'd had enough.

"Not even close, girls," I started. I wanted to say more, but tears were burning my eyes. The Darlings could push me around all they wanted, and I would stay strong, but bringing up Piggy was a low blow. "I have to go."

I took a step around them, clutching the bag tightly.

"We don't care what's in your stupid bag, Ryan!" Precious yelled as I walked away.

I was nearly out of earshot when I heard Lil say, "I bet it's her dress for the Beef Princess pageant!"

They burst into laughter at Lil's ridiculous suggestion, and I hurried down to the Feed and Seed. I felt the heat in my face rising with every step. It took a lot of nerve for the Darling sisters to speak to me about how to raise a steer.

I got the fly spray for $3.29 plus tax, and I headed back to meet Mom and Frannie. Mom thought the dress was just right.

"It's you, Libby!" she exclaimed when I showed it to her, but my own enthusiasm had been zapped.

When we got home, I stuffed the dress, bag and all, into the back of my dresser drawer. But before I went to bed, I got out the bag, smoothed the wrinkles out of the dress, and hung it in my closet. I wasn't going to let those three dumb Darlings ruin the perfect pageant dress or my desire to beat them. Within the next week, I would have two chances to put them in their places. Once in the show arena and once again in the pageant. And I just couldn't let them come away victorious in either one.

TWENTY

— off to the fair —

The first day of the Practical County Fair came as it always did. The big parade headed down Nowhere's Main Street and ended at the front gate of the fairgrounds, where Mayor Thompson made his opening comments and the marching band played and the Beef Princess, aka someone with the last name of Darling, fulfilled her first official fair duty and cut the ribbon, opening the fair to the public.

Mom, Frannie, and I had been in that crowd in recent years, keeping time with the band and cheering on Mayor Thompson, but this year, Mom and Frannie had to get along without me. I was way too busy packing the show box, rinsing Mule, and making final adjustments to the show equipment.

* * *

Earlier that morning Dad, Carol Ann, and I made a quick trip to the fairgrounds to set up Mule's stall in the beef barn. Carol Ann and I walked around the barn to see who was exhibiting. The Darling girls' "stuff" had already made an appearance. Three enormous pink and purple show boxes with DARLING FARMS across the top had been forklifted in the day before. The Darlings had staked out their position at the end of the barn most accessible to the public. Huge pink and purple polka-dotted banners hung over the stalls where their steers would stand mostly unattended all week while the two older Darlings giggled their way around the fairgrounds and Ohma growled if anyone so much as looked at her cross-eyed.

This year there were curtains to match the banners. I caught Carol Ann's eye as we watched Mrs. Darling nailing purple polka-dotted curtains to the walls above the windows near their stalls. Carol Ann gave me the I-think-I'm-going-to-gag look as we hurried past. We got away just in time. Behind us we could hear the arrival of the three Darling daughters. I glanced back in time to see Lil adjusting her sash and tiara. No doubt cutting the ribbon had been a difficult task.

Carol Ann and I hurried back to the other end of the beef barn, where bedding for Mule had been spread and Dad was setting up an enormous fan to keep him comfortable in the late-July heat.

"There we go," said Dad as he plugged the fan in and watched it whir until there was a good breeze going. He turned to Carol Ann and me.

"Looks like the fair is ready for Mule. You two ready to go with me to get him?"

"You bet," I answered. Being there and seeing the barns all prepared was exciting. I couldn't wait to get Mule settled in.

At home, Carol Ann and I spent a few minutes with Mule in his pen while Dad hitched the livestock trailer to the pickup.

"Are you ready to go to the fair, Mule?"

I spoke to him while Carol Ann braided his long, curly tail. At over twelve hundred pounds, he was tame as could be.

"Do you think he understands what you're saying, Libby?" Carol Ann asked.

"Probably not," I answered. "But he likes my voice. He always listens, whether he understands or not."

I brushed his side and rubbed behind his ears. I heard Dad backing the trailer up to the barn.

"This is it, Lib," Dad said as he opened the back of the trailer. I couldn't help but think of another time when the trailer had been in that same spot, and Piggy was the one being loaded. "Any doubts?"

Doubts? Of course I had doubts. This whole year had been about doubts. Back at Granddad's pasture last September I had doubted that Mule would amount to much, but just look at the awesome steer that stood before me now. I had doubted I'd ever like Mule half as much as Piggy, and he had won my heart.

"Actually, I think Mule is a fine steer. And he just may

be the best chance the Ryan family has ever had at Grand Champion. So, let's load him up and see how he does."

"That's my girl!" Dad patted me on the shoulder.

I led Mule into the back of the trailer. And we were off. Off to the Practical County Fair.

TWENTY-ONE

— a very long day —

The beef show didn't begin until the third day of the fair, so the second day was the perfect time for me to run around and see what there was to see. Carol Ann and I made our way to the midway as soon as morning chores in the beef barn were done.

The summer sun had the temperature well past eighty degrees by late morning. The Practical County Fair had a tendency to fall on the hottest days of the year.

Lots of people were on the fairgrounds already, probably taking in the sights before the afternoon heat set in. We saw Karen Elliott and found out she'd brought an Angus steer this year, too. We had to duck behind the Future Farmers of America tent to avoid Mr. Turner, the oldest, crabbiest math teacher at the middle school. We would see him soon enough when school started next month.

As we came around the front of the FFA tent, giggling and celebrating our successful avoidance of Mr. Turner, we ran smack-dab into Ohma Darling.

We stopped laughing.

"Watch where you're going, would you?" Ohma snapped.

"We're sorry," Carol Ann said sincerely. "We didn't see you there."

"Yeah, right," Ohma growled. "How can you miss me?"

She shoved right between Carol Ann and me, leaving us speechless for a minute.

"I swear," I said finally, "that girl is one of the grumpiest people I know."

"One of?"

"I wonder what makes her so unpleasant."

"I don't know," Carol Ann replied. "Maybe it's repressed anger from her childhood. Or a chemical imbalance. There have been studies, you know, that—"

"Carol Ann."

"What?"

"This is my day to have fun at the fair. Let's not analyze Ohma's social challenges."

Carol Ann agreed.

"Unless—"

"Oh, no you don't. The only thing I want to analyze is the positive effect of fair food on my mood!"

"Well, then, let's go!" Carol Ann suggested. "What should we try first? Funnel cakes? Deep-fried Twinkies?"

At noon we each bought an all-day ride pass. We agreed

that the Super Loop after funnel cakes might not be such a good idea, so we decided to try out something a little less nauseating: the bumper cars.

The line was short and the ride operator had already let some people on when we got to the bumper cars.

"You just made it," he told us, holding open the gate and motioning to the last two empty cars. We sat down and strapped ourselves in as the ride geared up.

I hit reverse in my sparkling green sports car just as Carol Ann did the same in her blue one, and our back bumpers tapped.

"I'm coming after you!" Carol Ann yelled over the noise of the ride, driving her car full speed ahead.

I quickly turned around and tried to get in behind her.

From out of nowhere, a red car smacked hard into my right side, knocking me sideways in my seat. I turned to see Precious Darling in huge white sunglasses, and she was backing up to hit me again.

No way was I going to let her do that. I made a quick turn and scanned the bumper cars for Carol Ann. I couldn't believe my eyes. She was in the corner, wedged between the railings and two cars, driven by none other than Ohma and Lil! How dare they go after my best friend?

"I'm coming, Carol Ann!" I hollered.

Carol Ann was frantically trying to reverse her vehicle, but it was no use. Every time she backed up even an inch, the cars belonging to both Darlings shoved her back into the corner.

I planned my attack carefully. Lil would be easier to knock away than Ohma, so I headed straight for Lil's silver car. I was right. She saw me coming and screamed, putting her car into reverse to avoid me. That left an open shot at Ohma's purple car. Carol Ann was finally free from the corner, so she spun around and headed after Lil, who could be heard shrieking, "No, no! Don't hit me! No!"

Ohma was making a getaway, glancing over her shoulder. She knew I was behind her. I was almost there, ready to knock her good, when I was slammed from the right.

Ugh! It was Vicious Darling again in her white shades and red car. I backed up and saw Carol Ann motion to me to head her way. I don't know if Carol Ann's amazing mind engineered what happened next, or if we simply got incredibly lucky, but as Carol Ann sped toward me with Lil on her tail, I drove straight toward Carol Ann with Precious and Ohma on mine. When we were just inches apart, I heard her yell "Left!" so I whipped my car in one direction at the same moment she veered in the other.

What resulted was head-on Darling devastation. Lil and Precious smacked so hard, Precious's sunglasses flew onto the floor. Ohma had no time to avoid her sisters and hit Precious at full speed, but not before obliterating the sunglasses. The ride operator cut power to all cars as Carol Ann and I did a drive-by high five.

When the whine of the ride ended and everyone got out of their seat belts and cars, the sisters' bickering could be heard loud and clear.

"Shut up, stupid."

"You shut up. You owe me a pair of sunglasses."

"Do not, idiot."

"I broke a nail!"

Carol Ann and I left the ride laughing hysterically. That was the most fun I'd had in a while. It sure felt good to encounter the Darlings and come out on top for once! It was definitely a feeling I could get used to.

Back in the beef barn, we gave Mule fresh water and positioned his fan on him. Heat like this was hard on the animals. The heat, along with the move from home to the fair, could stress out a steer.

I had intended to go out the back door of the barn to avoid the Darling Farms exhibit and a possible run-in with the Mr. and Mrs., but I forgot until it was too late. We were headed straight for the polka-dotted curtains with a crowd of fairgoers behind us. We had no choice.

It appeared we were lucky, because the Darling steers were lined up, three in a row beneath the pink and purple name signs, with not a soul around. We hesitated a moment to check them out. Ever since the Darlings showed up at Ryansmeade that evening last fall, bragging about their steers, I'd been curious to see just what they would bring to the Practical County Fair.

Looking at the three animals before us, I wasn't very impressed. Precious's steer was jet-black, although his hair didn't have near the sheen Mule's had. He had a little white spot right in the middle of his forehead, which I thought looked just like the shape of Ohio. He looked a little underweight for a market animal. Lil's steer was a reddish brown and white Hereford who desperately needed a good brushing and probably a good feeding as well. Ohma's steer, surprisingly, looked to be the best of the bunch. Maybe she had actually given hers a little attention. Still, he wasn't very well proportioned for a show steer. He wasn't anything to brag about, in my opinion.

Carol Ann was surveying the three animals with a puzzled look.

"Well, admittedly, I know very little about the bovine species, but don't these steers look pitiful to you?"

"It's typical," I explained. "The Darlings don't spend any time with their animals before or during the fair."

"And these girls are the crowned spokeswomen for the beef industry? That's pathetic!" Carol Ann cried. "*Someone* ought to do something about that!"

"I don't see *you* signing up for a pageant, Carol Ann," I teased. Between my best friend and my mother, I wasn't sure who wanted me in that Beef Princess pageant more. Ugh. I hadn't given the pageant much thought lately, and just mentioning it made my stomach turn.

"Let's go."

I started to leave, but stopped when I noticed Ohma's steer.

"Look," I said.

"Look at what?"

"Ohma's steer. See how his stomach is so round on the left side?"

Carol Ann leaned forward.

"I guess. What's that mean?"

"It could mean that he's bloated. And that's not good."

"What do you think you're doing?"

The voice came from behind us. I turned to see Precious, arms folded, mouth open, eyelashes batting.

"This steer—" I started.

"That steer is my sister's, and what did you do to it?" Precious said accusingly.

"I didn't do anything to it, but I think it's getting sick."

"It's not sick. It's fine. Now get out of here!"

Carol Ann was already halfway out the door. I followed, but turned one last time. I knew for a fact that I had more knowledge about steers in my pinky toe than Precious had in her whole pea brain. I wasn't going to let her intimidate me.

"Precious, listen to me. You need to call the vet. That steer isn't well and needs to be looked at . . . *soon*."

"Oh, really?" Precious scoffed. "And who made you junior veterinarian? You know, Libby Ryan, I really don't give a flip what you think you know about steers, okay?"

I'd said what I could. Precious wasn't going to listen to me. She was probably still miffed about her sunglasses.

Carol Ann and I spent the rest of the day watching the horse show at the grandstand. We ate and laughed and finally rode the Super Loop. Twice. Then we decided twice might have been one too many times.

By dusk we had checked in with my parents and convinced them that we all needed one ride on the Ferris wheel after dark, because the fair isn't the fair until you've seen it at night, with all its colored lights, from the top of the Ferris wheel.

I climbed into a red gondola car with Carol Ann while my parents got into a green one behind us with Frannie on the seat between them. Better to have Frannie with my parents, and not with Carol Ann and me. That child was just so unpredictable.

Once around to let passengers out and others in and finally we were off, spinning through the night air, a blur of color before us. Up and around, I closed my eyes and savored the coming down, my favorite part. Again and again. I looked back to see Frannie clapping her hands while Mom and Dad each kept a hand planted firmly on her shoulders. We slowed, and I knew the ride was almost over.

We were stopped at the top when I noticed several trucks in front of the beef barns. Only emergency vehicles were allowed on the fairgrounds. I turned to Dad behind me and pointed in the direction of the barns. The music and crowd drowned out his reply, but as soon as we were all on the ground again, we headed in that direction.

"What do you think is going on?" I asked, nearly running to keep up with Dad.

"We'll see soon enough," came Dad's reply. The look of concern on his face said more than his words.

We entered the barn from the back to avoid the crowd at the front. I breathed a sigh of relief when I saw Mule comfortably lying in the straw, securely fastened in his spot.

Jack Evans's father walked toward us.

"What's going on, Dave?" Dad asked.

"It's that youngest Darling girl's steer. It's dead."

No sooner had Jack's dad delivered the news about Ohma's steer than Precious and Lil appeared, hurling accusations my way.

"There she is! That Libby Ryan was hanging around my

sister's steer this afternoon! She *poisoned* him or something," Precious shrieked so that the entire barn could hear.

I was speechless. How could she think I would hurt an animal? Even Ohma's.

Carol Ann, who was never at a loss for words, and multi-syllabic ones at that, stepped forward.

"Now, listen to reason, would you, Precious?"

I imagined it was nearly killing Carol Ann to call Precious by her first name, but she let it glide off her tongue like it was nothing at all.

"Are you even aware of the multitude of diseases that can attack the bovine species? Not to mention the stress of cohabiting in such close quarters with numerous other animals in the heat of summer? When it comes to what could have killed your sister's steer, a thousand different scenarios come to mind, and not one of them includes Libby Ryan!"

Wow. Now I was even more speechless. I just stared at Carol Ann, once again astounded by her loyalty. What a friend.

"Well," Lil huffed, "I'll have you know my baby sister is devastated. She's been crying all evening."

Okay, that was enough to rock my voice into action.

"Devastated? Are you kidding? I have never seen one of you show any concern for any of your animals!"

I could have gone on, but Dad was giving me one of his be-careful-what-you-say looks.

"Of course she's upset!" Precious spoke again. "After all, you do realize that now she has no steer. And no steer means no auction! Think of all the money she's lost!"

Precious didn't wait for a reply. She turned and huffed off. Lil scurried to keep up with her.

I was angry enough to spit! Money. That was all the divas of Darling Farms could think about! Money was the only reason they showed steers in the first place. But the worst part of it all was that those girls had the nerve to say such awful things about me when they had no concern whatsoever for their animals.

Other exhibitors stood around the barn, whispering and looking my way. Could they possibly believe I would hurt Ohma's steer? My mind flashed back to the day outside the thrift store, when Lil mentioned that Piggy had died. If the word around town was that I had poisoned Piggy . . .

I felt tears stinging my eyes.

"Dad . . ."

"Hey, listen, Lib," Dad said. "I saw Susan's truck pull up to the other end of the barn a few minutes ago. She's down there now, and she'll be able to straighten this whole thing out with one look at Ohma's steer. Besides, everyone in this barn knows how well, or how poorly, the Darling family cares for their livestock. Don't worry."

It was getting late and we still needed to bed Mule down for the night. Just then Mom and Frannie appeared inside the barn door.

"Just checking to see if everything's all right," Mom said.

Dad nodded.

"We'll fill you in at home. From the looks of it, you'd better head that way soon."

Flopped over Mom's shoulder, in her brown jacket,

Frannie looked like a stuffed teddy bear. A teddy bear that had just devoured pink cotton candy.

"I'm tired," she whined, wrapping her sticky fingers around Mom's neck, narrowly missing her hair.

"Okay, we're going. Carol Ann, it looks like Libby and Mr. Ryan are going to be a while. Want me to drop you at home?"

Carol Ann turned to me.

"Are you all right?"

"Yeah. I'm fine."

"Okay, then, I'll head out with your mom. But I'll be back tomorrow for the big event."

"Okay," I said.

Then, before she got to the door, I added, "Thanks, Carol Ann."

She gave me a smile and a wave before she said to my mom, "Here, Mrs. Ryan, I'll carry Frannie for you."

There was no doubt about it. Carol Ann Cuthbert was a saint.

The commotion at the other end of the barn was over by the time we got Mule settled in for the night. Susan's truck was gone and the fair board had seen to it that Ohma's steer was promptly removed. It was not good for public relations to have dead livestock lying around when people came through the barns.

As we walked past the pink and purple palace, Precious's and Lil's steers were both settled for the night, but no humans were hanging around. I had a sad feeling when I looked at the empty spot where Ohma's steer had been hours earlier. I felt strangely sorry for Ohma. I'd lost Piggy, but under different circumstances. I simply could not imagine what it would be like to lose Mule after all the months of time and work I had invested in preparing him for show.

Of course, I *would* lose Mule, and I knew it, and I had known it all along. It was part of the project. The circle of life. The perpetuation of the food chain. Dad had a thousand ways of putting it. And as much as I hated to lose Mule, it was going to happen.

So why, if all these steers were destined to end up on someone's table, was my heart breaking for Ohma? She wasn't, after all, the friendliest girl I'd ever met, was she?

I don't know if I would have ever known the answer to those questions if it hadn't been for a couple of red hair ribbons.

TWENTY-TWO

— a strange encounter —

Dad and I were walking slowly to the truck at the far end of the livestock exhibitors' lot. The midway had shut down for the night, the fairgoers had gone home, and the only people remaining were the livestock folks like us. I was exhausted and grimy from the heat of the day and the dust of the fair. I was thinking about a refreshing shower and washing the dirt out of my hair.

That was when I remembered.

"Dad, I have to go back."

He looked at me. It had been a long day, and it showed in every line on his tired face.

"Why?" He sighed an I'm-trying-to-be-patient sigh.

"Because I have two red hair ribbons in the show box

that Karen Elliott is letting me borrow for tomorrow. And Mom's going to braid my hair at home in the morning before the show. I have to have them, Dad."

"Okay, you go back. I'll walk out to the truck and pull up to the barn to pick you up."

"Thanks, Dad! I'll hurry."

The braids had been Carol Ann's idea. No ponytail for a cattlewoman, she had insisted. *Real* cattlewomen wore braids. No doubt, she'd been reading too much historical fiction lately.

I did hurry. I was a little creeped out about the silence of the fairgrounds at night. It was unnatural. A fair was supposed to be an active, noisy place with rides running and animal sounds and carnival workers shouting to pull in their next customers. At that hour it was all too still.

Mule barely blinked as I ruffled through the show box. It didn't take but a second to snatch the ribbons from the tray where I'd left them. I hurried to the end of the empty barn to wait for Dad. No headlights coming my way yet. I leaned up against the barn siding just outside the Darling Farms exhibit. And that was when I heard it.

Snuffling. Or snorting. I honestly thought maybe a stray hog had wandered over from the pig barn, but in the shadows I could see nothing. Yet the noise only got louder, so I went back into the barn. There, alone in the dark, sitting in the straw where her steer had been, was Ohma Darling.

"Hi," I offered.

I wasn't sure what else to say. If I tried to talk to her, would she rip me apart for allegedly killing her fair steer?

"Hi," came her grumbled reply.

It was silent until she snuffled again. Why was she sitting in the barn all alone at this hour? In the dim light it was hard to tell if she had been crying.

"I'm really sorry about what happened to your steer," I said, hoping she wouldn't take my sympathy as some sort of admission of guilt.

"What do you know about it?" she asked flatly. I wasn't sure if she was accusing me or questioning me.

I took a cautious step closer to her.

"Ohma, I promise I didn't do anything to your steer. I saw him this afternoon, and I told your sister to call the vet. I'm so sorry."

"I know that," she said.

"You do?" I asked. I wasn't very good at hiding my surprise.

"Yeah. Dr. Susan said he died from eating too much feed. And the wrong kind. Lil fed him. And then I fed him. I gave him feed from that bag over there."

She pointed to the Evanses' exhibit. I knew how important it was to feed consistently. Messing with feed can cause an animal to bloat and even die. I had been right after all.

I glanced in the direction of the parking lot. Dad didn't seem to be on his way yet.

"Can I sit down?" I asked.

"I don't care," she mumbled. Then she added, "If you want. You don't have to."

I sat. In all my years of going to school with Ohma, she and I had never had a real conversation. She was usually just so unpleasant to be around.

I glanced at Ohma. She really did look devastated. And I had a feeling it wasn't all about money.

Then, to my surprise, she began to cry.

"I killed Roberto."

"Roberto?"

"That was his name."

"Oh."

"I was too stupid to take care of my own animal!"

Her loud voice rocked the empty barn, and again, I wasn't sure what to do. I put my arm around her shoulder.

"It's okay," I told her. "I know how you feel."

"No, you don't," she said, a look of disbelief on her face.

"Yeah, I do. The steer I brought to the fair wasn't even supposed to be my fair calf. I had two, remember? The other one was the one that I liked better at first. And one day last spring, he got hurt. Every single day I wonder if I should have checked on him earlier, or wired the gate tighter, or done something to protect him."

She nodded as though she knew exactly what I was saying.

"He was counting on me to take good care of him, and I let him down," I finished.

"I really tried to take care of Roberto," Ohma said softly. "You have no idea what it's like."

No idea what it's like to care for a steer? Of course I knew all about that, but Ohma was talking about something entirely different.

"I can't live up to my sisters," she continued. "I mean, look at me. I'm nothing like them."

It was a well-known fact. Ohma was not petite, not gorgeous, not anything like her sisters. It must not have been an easy task, trying to live up to their expectations.

"I thought if I could do well in the steer show it might make up for the way I'm sure I'll bomb in the Beef Princess pageant," she said matter-of-factly.

She sobbed again, a little more quietly, and we sat for a while. The mystery of Ohma Darling was starting to unravel. She didn't hate the world, like her grouchiness had led us all to believe. She despised herself.

"I decided to be in the Beef Princess pageant this year, too," I reminded her. "And I don't feel very much like a beauty queen, either."

Ohma turned toward me, and I thought I saw a hint of a smile on her face.

"It was my mom's idea," I continued. "She thought it would be a good experience."

"You should see my dress," Ohma confided. "It's the white one Lil wore three years ago. I look like a giant marshmallow in it."

I smiled.

"I think I tried on a hundred dresses before I finally found one I liked. And you want to know something? I did get it at the thrift store in town."

"Really? Yours isn't new, either?"

"Nope. And, besides, I had to *buy* my used dress because *nothing* in Ronnie's closet was suitable for the Beef Princess pageant!"

"Well, I'd hope not!" Ohma nearly giggled. Who would have thought it could happen?

172

We shared a laugh until the rumble of Dad's diesel engine pickup approached.

"Need a ride?" I asked.

"I guess so," Ohma answered.

"I'm sure my dad will drop you at home."

We stood and brushed the straw off our jeans, and I opened the door to the truck. I slid in next to Dad, who gave me a what's-this-all-about look, and Ohma sat by the window. As Dad backed up, the truck's headlights lit up the open end of the barn again, briefly illuminating the empty spot where Roberto had been.

I saw Ohma quickly wipe away a tear before it could fall down her cheek. The painful memory of seeing Piggy's pen the day after he'd been taken away came rushing back, and I squeezed Ohma's hand as a tear fell down my own cheek.

TWENTY-THREE

— chaos in the ring —

On the day of the show, Dad and I left the farm chores to Granddad and Ronnie so that we could get to the fairgrounds early. Mom braided my hair in two short braids and tied Karen's ribbons on each one just as the sun was coming up. I grabbed my best jeans, the striped shirt we'd bought for the show, a belt, and my boots, and I was out the door.

At the fair, Mule ate a hearty breakfast of grain and hay before we led him to the wash racks to clean him up good. After that, we took him to a grooming chute and brushed and sprayed his thick, coal-black coat until he looked like a stuffed black bear. It occurred to me that we'd spent more time on Mule's hair that morning than I usually spent on mine in a month.

Dad had fastened the paper exhibitor number to my back with safety pins just as the announcer called for Mule's class of steers to enter the arena. The arena consisted of a big building with a large ring of metal gates in the center and bleachers on either side. A huge announcer's box with a microphone sat right in the center. It was a noisy, busy place with steers and exhibitors coming and going from the ring while the announcer's voice bounced off the building's metal roof and siding.

Now, with the stands full of family, friends, and curious fairgoers, the steer show had begun. Mom, Granddad, Carol Ann, and Ronnie sat together in the front row. Then there was Frannie, with a space just big enough for the grand-children between her and Ronnie.

Ten exhibitors, including Karen Elliott and her Angus and Lil Darling and her Hereford, were in Mule's weight class. Jim Darling's daughters might have been used to being winners on the stage, but in the arena, they had a much different track record. That Hereford would be easy to beat.

We filed into the arena and got to work setting up our steers. I gave Mule a gentle nudge with the show stick to set his back hooves in the proper position. A quick check of the back. Everything was perfect. Good. Now, to keep it all just so, I used a steady, rhythmic rubbing of his underbelly with the show stick. Mule blinked, but he didn't move a muscle.

The judge hesitated in front of Mule. My heart raced. *It's just the same as we practiced at home*, I told myself. *Pretend the judge is Ronnie. Pretend we're standing in the barnyard.* Oh, my heart never pounded like this in the barnyard. This was for real!

I froze as the judge eyed Mule. Only after he moved on down the line did I exhale and relax slightly, remembering not to take my eyes off him. It was a rule that at that very moment Lil Darling wasn't following.

The judge stopped in front of her steer. Obviously daydreaming, Lil was suddenly jerked back to reality as her steer reared his head back, spooked by the judge's slight touch on the nose. Lil snapped to attention, yanking roughly on the halter and using her show stick like a cattle prod. Her steer bolted forward, the audience gasped, and Mr. Fields from the Cattlemen's Club leaped into action to help her get the animal under control.

I caught the whole thing from the corner of my eye, never taking my attention from Mule. I whispered softly in his ear, telling him what a fine job he was doing, all the while remaining keenly aware of the judge's movements.

After several minutes and with much assistance from Mr. Fields, Lil and her steer were back in line. Lil looked disgusted, the animal looked impatient, and the judge looked completely unimpressed.

Lil's control of her steer didn't last long. As she was picking at her fuchsia fingernail polish, her scraggly Hereford lurched forward. She jerked hard on his halter and muttered something I couldn't hear in his ear, but I was willing to bet it wasn't very complimentary.

Suddenly, the steer leaped out of line and bolted across the show ring, spooking several others with his wild motion. Instantly, there was chaos in the ring. Around me, everyone else was struggling to keep control of their own situation. Lil's steer had set off a chain reaction.

"It's okay," I told Mule, who never flinched but instead blinked his long eyelashes as if to say, "I know."

Running and kicking wildly, Lil's steer made a complete circle around the ring with Lil still hanging on to his lead rope, screaming for help.

"Don't you let go, girl!" I heard Mr. Darling command as the men from the Cattlemen's Club dashed into the ring to rescue Lil.

"Let go, baby! Let go before that thing hurts you, sugar!"

That was Mrs. Darling yelling from the stands. I caught a glimpse of her peeking out from behind her own fuchsia fingernails as her hands covered her face in horror.

Precious stood in the bleachers and shouted, "Don't let him drag you, Lil. Those are my jeans you're wearing!"

Beside her sat Ohma, looking somewhat unsympathetic to her older sister's plight. She looked directly at me, and just as I was about to smile at her, an enormous crash turned all heads to the far end of the arena.

Lil's steer had jumped the gate and was headed toward the midway, leaving Lil sprawled in the sawdust. The other exhibitors circled their nervous animals around the ring, the roar of Mr. Darling's voice echoed through the show arena, and Mrs. Darling grabbed a reluctant Ohma to go help Lil.

"What'd you let go for?" Mr. Darling bellowed.

Lil was in tears, rubbing the rope burns on her palms. Her father didn't even wait for an answer as he jumped the gate and joined the other men who had gone to try to bring the steer back.

Lil was in her mother's doting care when the announcer called for everyone's attention and the judge resumed the show. He gave us the signal to walk. *Here goes nothing,* I thought. I tucked the show stick under my arm and pulled with both hands as hard as I could.

Mule's big blue eyes met mine and with a slow blink he took a hesitant first step and then another and another. He was walking! Mule, my stubborn steer, was doing just as he was supposed to just when he was supposed to.

"Good fella, good guy," I praised him as I returned my gaze to the judge.

Twice around the ring with Emmett Erickson's fuzzy red and white Shorthorn on my tail, and the judge gave us the motion to stop. Now, "Stop" was a command I knew Mule would obey.

I set him up, all four hooves in perfect position. Lifting his head, I stepped behind him so that the judge could get one final look at his long body, muscular shoulders, and perfect back.

Just then the judge motioned me to the center of the ring. A hush fell over the arena as I silently pleaded with Mule to move. As if he'd read my mind, he set off for the center of the ring just as soon as I pulled on his halter.

My mind raced as I set up Mule again in the center of the ring. Had the judge liked my steer? He put Karen Elliott and her Angus beside me.

The audience was silent except for a few whispers each time the judge placed another exhibitor. Everyone was speculating, trying to guess what was going on in the judge's mind.

Mule remained patient. I glanced from Mule to the judge and back again, but once when I looked up, I saw Dad.

TWENTY-FOUR

— a fair fight —

With Mule back in the beef barn, munching on a reward of grain and hay, my family and I took a seat in the bleachers to watch the other weight classes. The winners of these would be my competition in the final round.

The next weight class to come out into the ring was a good-looking group of steers slightly smaller than Mule. As they entered one by one, I began to evaluate each steer in my mind. There were two I could dismiss immediately. Second one, too thin. Fourth one, a little fat for his frame. That left five others that all looked great to me. I began to appreciate how difficult it must be for the judge to sort out these animals.

Granddad whispered, "I'm going with the Shorthorn."

I took a long look at Josh Joseph's red and white steer. The Josephs' Shorthorns were known throughout the Midwest, and Josh had raised a nice-looking one to show this year.

Minutes later, the judge was greeting Josh Joseph with a congratulatory handshake. Granddad had called it right, as usual.

As the judge lined up the next class, Dad returned with a box that smelled so wonderful I knew what was in it before he even opened it. Cattlemen's burgers, hot and juicy. There was only one week a year to savor those one-third-pound, one hundred percent Grade A lean beef burgers. The rest of the year, a person could only savor the memory and dream of the next Practical County Fair.

Why didn't I wait until after the fair to become a vegetarian? I moaned to myself. I was starving. I hadn't eaten a thing before the show. Dad passed the burgers down the row of bleachers, and one by one I sent them on until everyone had one but me.

"You gonna eat?" Dad asked.

"Naw, not right now," I said with a shrug.

He shook his head but didn't say another word. I turned my head toward the arena, hoping to catch a whiff of sawdust and manure. Anything to get my mind off those burgers.

Jack Evans won the heavyweight class with a monster of an Angus.

"Whoa." Carol Ann drew in her breath. "That one is *massive*."

Yeah, no kidding, I thought. *A massive threat to Mule in the final round.*

The last class of steers was the lightest class. Precious Darling's thin little Angus with the white Ohio-shaped spot would be in this class, along with some other smaller but nicer-looking animals. As they entered the ring, Precious pulled her small black steer along, flashing her brightest smile at the judge. Her show clothes were perfect, her hair sprayed so it wouldn't move an inch in the draft of the fans. If she couldn't impress the judge with her steer, she was hoping to win him over with her stunning good looks.

Precious set up her steer. How had that calf learned to stand so well? Lil's animal was so wild it took three men to keep it in the ring, and even they had failed. And Precious's steer stood perfectly on command? I doubted that she had spent a single minute more in the barn all year than her sister had.

"Hey, Libby," Carol Ann said. "When we saw that calf in the beef barn the other day, wasn't his hair a lot messier?"

"Yeah," I agreed as Precious passed by us with her spotless steer. It would take weeks of washing and brushing to make a steer's hair that shiny and smooth. Something was up.

But another thing was bothering me. Of all the lightweight steers out there, Precious Darling's was the best-looking.

Granddad whispered, "It's gonna be the Angus."

The judge walked to the microphone.

"These calves are just a little smaller framed than the rest of those shown here today, but there's one out here that you just have to like for the muscle he's got on him despite his smaller size, and that's this smiling young lady's steer right here in front of me."

The applause in the arena was nearly drowned out by the whispers in the crowd. One of Jim Darling's daughters had a class winner after all these years of Darlings being at the bottom.

"Who would have thought?" Dad commented later that evening when we got Mule ready for his second show.

The hot breeze of the afternoon had settled, leaving us with a still, humid night. Flies buzzed around Mule's head as I used the last of the fly spray on his neck.

"There's another can in the truck," Dad told me.

"I'll be back in a bit," I replied.

There was something going on with Precious Darling's steer, but I wasn't sure what. I thought about it as I walked out across the field of parked trucks and empty livestock and horse trailers.

That was when I heard something coming from the trailers. It sounded like a long, low moo.

There shouldn't be any livestock this far from the barns, I thought.

Had a steer gotten loose? I had to move closer to listen better, so I took a few more steps toward the lot. Just then, a shadow moved across the trailer to my right, so I quietly slipped behind a pickup truck and peeked up over the bed. I couldn't believe my eyes.

It was Jim Darling, walking up to a parked stock trailer. Mr. Darling opened the back of the trailer, revealing a black steer inside. I watched breathlessly as he gave it some feed and water and then jumped out of the trailer, closed the door tightly, and walked away toward the beef barn.

It was all starting to make sense. Precious's surprise win, her steer's sudden makeover. But there was only one way I could be sure. I stole from one trailer to the next until I was standing right beside the red trailer marked DARLING FARMS. I could hear the steer moving around inside.

I looked around quickly, and seeing no one, I stepped up onto the wheel cover on the side of the trailer. Peering through the metal slats, I could see the steer with his head bent over his feed pan. Even in the dim light, I could see that his mottled fur was anything but well groomed. I clicked my tongue twice to get his attention. I needed to see his face to be sure. Then he lifted his head and turned to face me, still chewing, hay hanging out of both sides of his mouth.

There before me was the proof. *This* was the black calf with the small white spot in the shape of Ohio on his forehead. If this was the steer Precious Darling had brought to the fair, then the one in the show today, the one in the barn now, must have come from somewhere else.

"Libby Ryan!"

The voice startled me so that I lost my footing and fell squarely on my butt in the grass.

"What are you doing?"

It was Precious who had caught me looking into the trailer. From my point of view there on the ground, she looked older, taller, and more intimidating than ever.

"I, um, I . . ."

Think fast, Libby. Think fast.

Why was I so nervous? She was one who'd just been caught cheating. She was the one who should be shaking in her pointy-toed pink boots.

I stood and looked her in the eye. I knew the truth, and she couldn't lie her way out of it.

"You switched steers, didn't you?"

"I did not," Precious lied.

"You did. I saw your steer the first day of the fair. He was a scraggly-looking thing with a white spot on his forehead."

"So? Maybe I cleaned him up good. Everyone cleans up their animals for show, Libby. You know that."

She was going to try her best to talk her way out of the corner she'd put herself in.

"No, Precious, I know that's not true, because the first steer, the one you really raised, is right here in this trailer. Where'd you get the other one? My guess is that your daddy paid a whole lot for it not all that long ago. Say, yesterday, maybe? After you got here and realized that the competition was just too tough for your own neglected steers to stand up against?"

I had her now. I could see it in the look on her face and the way she opened her mouth and nothing came out. I had just one more thing to say.

"I am going to the Cattlemen's Club right this minute and telling them that you've been cheating. You'll lose your class winner, and your entire family will be banned from showing at the Practical County Fair this year and next year, too."

I was standing up to Precious Darling, and it felt great. There was almost nothing she could say now.

Almost.

Precious Darling seemed fazed for only a minute before she shook her long blond hair, batted her long fake eyelashes, and leaned in close to me.

"Libby Ryan, you hear this," she hissed. "You may think you have things all figured out, but let me tell you that if you so much as breathe one word of your suspicions to anyone"—she was right up in my face now; I had no idea what was coming next—"I will tell all of Practical County that your stupid, sorry excuse for a pageant gown came from a thrift store."

I stared at her. I liked my dress. I didn't care where it came from, or who knew it, for that matter. I opened my mouth to tell her, but Precious wasn't done.

"Have you ever even *been* to a pageant, Libby?"

I didn't answer. I hadn't. It wasn't exactly the part of the fair that had appealed to me in the past.

"Do you have any idea what you're getting yourself into?"

Again, I didn't know what to say.

"I didn't think so." She smirked. "Let me tell you this much. Pageants are for *pretty* girls, Libby. The judges look for poise. And *beauty*. They pick girls who stand out onstage. Not tomboys who need the scholarship money."

I hated to think that she might possibly know what she was talking about. But, of course, she did. She held the record for having won the pageant more often than any other girl in Practical County.

"And let me tell you what the others will be wearing. Gorgeous, name-brand evening gowns from department stores in Fort Wayne or Indianapolis. Not cheap, pathetic little dresses from secondhand stores."

I was speechless. The triumph showed on her face.

"Oh, don't worry, Libby. Your dress will be fine," she said sarcastically. "I just hope something doesn't happen to it before the big night."

Was she threatening to mess with my dress before the pageant? I had no doubt she would stoop to something so drastic. She knew I had nothing else I could possibly wear.

"Well, I guess that settles it, then." She glared. And with that she stomped off toward the beef barn, leaving me dumbfounded.

TWENTY-FIVE

— the final drive —

The exhibitors and their animals left the beef barn one by one and entered the ring where the judge already paced. First I noticed the stands. There were so many more people here this evening than there had been this afternoon. Dad was standing at the end of the arena with a few other anxious fathers. My eyes searched the bleachers. Mom and Ronnie and Frannie. Granddad. Carol Ann was there. Mayor Thompson and Dr. Susan. And my dentist. It seemed like all of Nowhere had turned out for the final round of the beef show.

So far, Mule was walking well. Calm, cool Mule.

Suddenly the exhibitor in front of me stopped, and Mule nearly rear-ended Josh's Shorthorn.

Pay attention, I thought. *Focus.*

I'd had very little time to consider what to do about Precious Darling, her cheating, and her threats. My first plan had been to turn in Precious and quit the pageant. But my goal since I decided to enter had been to make sure another Darling didn't represent the cattle farmers of Practical County for another year. I couldn't win if I didn't even try.

My second thought, and probably the one that burned me the most, was of Ohma. I had befriended her the night her steer died, and she had betrayed me by telling her sisters about my dress. How could I have been so dumb as to trust a Darling? I'd thought Ohma was different from her sisters, but it sure looked like I was wrong.

At some point while I brushed and haltered Mule for the evening's competition, I decided to keep my mouth shut and see how the final round of the beef show went with Precious in it. I was still sure Mule could beat her, even with her counterfeit steer.

So there we stood. Josh Joseph with his Shorthorn, Jack Evans with his enormous Angus, Precious with her impostor, and me with Mule. Four class winners battling it out in the final drive for Grand and Reserve Champion Steer at the Practical County Fair.

Mule let me set him up without so much as a wiggle on his part. The same judge had returned, wearing the same green boots, but in a tan shirt this time. He was slowly making his way down the line.

Hold still, I told Mule without speaking. A tap here, a rub there. I could tell him exactly what I wanted. My nervousness had been spent on the first round. Being out in the ring with Mule now felt like second nature. We were a team. A superduo, Mule and I.

Without warning, a sad, crushing feeling came over me. It was the same feeling that had kept me awake late on those hot, sticky summer nights. It was the same feeling that had led to my completely irrational decision to open the back gate on the Fourth of July. It was a feeling that had the power to bring tears in a heartbeat.

I clenched my teeth, blinked once, and concentrated on the judge, determined that if Mule didn't win this show, it wouldn't be for lack of showmanship on my part. The judge stopped and motioned for me to step out of line and circle the ring with Mule. After a brief hesitation, Mule stepped out in great form.

As I passed the bleachers, I couldn't help noticing the Darling family perched in the very front row. Ohma was trying to catch my eye, and she gave me a small smile. I looked away. I wasn't going to trust her ever again.

I noticed that Jack looked pretty confident when he walked his steer in front of the judge. When Precious pranced by me with a triumphant smile, I saw the white spot on her animal's forehead. For crying out loud, it looked more like California than Ohio! How could they think no one would notice they'd made a switch? One more look at Precious's smug face, and I was starting to regret my decision to keep quiet.

The judge was coming back. The audience waited silently while he ran his hands along the side of each animal.

A turn of the judge's hand and we all rotated our steers,

this time so the judge was looking them square in the hind end. I prayed Mule wouldn't lift his tail and leave a pile of crap at the judge's feet.

One last turn and we were looking at the judge again. The sun had set an hour ago, but the heat of the Indiana July night was almost unbearable. Under the lights of the arena and the tension of the show, it was amazing that Precious Darling's makeup was holding up as well as it was. I was sweating like crazy, and I thought it might be interesting to see Precious's face melt into gooey globs of pink blush and blue eye shadow.

All at once, the judge was at the microphone. He hadn't even lined us up yet. I wondered what that meant.

With a crisp white handkerchief, he wiped the sweat from his brow.

"I'd like to thank you folks for having me here in Practical County tonight."

You're welcome.

"I've got to say, ladies and gentlemen, I thought your young exhibitors put on a real great show here in the arena this afternoon . . ."

Okay, you said that earlier.

". . . but tonight, well, there's no denying you've got some of the state's top steers in the ring. And with that, you've got some top-notch showmen in these young exhibitors. Let's give them a round of applause for their hard work."

I glanced at Precious, who was now basking in the applause that she so totally didn't deserve. She glared back at me. I could see Mom and Frannie clapping. Granddad had moved over to stand with Dad near the gate. My arm was really tired from the constant motion of the show stick, and even Mule, the calmest steer on the planet, was starting to fidget.

"Folks, I'm going to pick you a Grand Champion Steer."

A hush came over the place as the judge took one last, long look. Jack's steer let out a loud, impatient bellow, which broke the tension and caused a ripple of laughter to echo through the audience. With nervous anticipation, the arena fell silent once again.

The judge circled each pair of animals and exhibitors. He paused in front of Precious's steer and studied him from all angles. He sucked in his breath and held it in his cheeks, as if he was giving serious consideration to the small black steer held by Precious.

If he picked Precious's steer for Grand Champion, I would regret for the rest of my life not turning her in for cheating. One more look at all four steers, and the judge made a move toward Precious.

I held my breath. I couldn't look.

A squeal of the microphone made everyone, including the judge, look in the direction of the announcer's stand. Mr. Fields, president of the Cattlemen's Club, held the microphone.

"Ladies and gentlemen, I'm sorry to interrupt the competition at such an intense moment, but it has just come to my attention that one of these exhibitors has been disqualified from competition."

There were gasps and murmurs throughout the bleachers. Before Mr. Fields could even announce her name, Precious was protesting.

"What? That's not true!"

That was when I saw Ohma standing at Mr. Fields's side. I couldn't believe it. She had turned her sister in to the Cattlemen. She looked sick, and I knew it must have been a difficult thing to do. I also knew that the flak she would likely suffer from the rest of her family wouldn't be pretty.

"Precious, you will need to take your steer out of the arena," Mr. Fields said as he leaned over the announcer's stand, his hand covering the microphone. He was trying his best to spare her as much humiliation as possible. But it wasn't in the nature of the Darling family to bow quietly out of anything. Mr. and Mrs. Darling were on their feet, shouting at Mr. Fields. Two other gentlemen from the Cattlemen's Club escorted a defiant Precious and her steer out of the ring.

The judge and Mr. Fields held a hushed conversation while the stands buzzed in reaction to Precious Darling's disqualification.

I patted Mule's side, which by now was wet with perspiration. He was being so patient. At the far end of the arena, I saw Ohma, and she appeared to be getting an earful from an irate Lil. I couldn't believe Ohma had had the courage to do what was right. She'd been braver than I had. I hoped I would get a chance to talk to her before her family dragged her away to face whatever punishment they would dole out for doing the right thing.

But that would have to wait. The judge was back in the arena. He gave ample attention to each of the three remaining steers but seemed to make up his mind rather quickly.

He walked to the center of the ring, paused just briefly enough for the audience to draw in their breath in suspense, and made a beeline toward Josh Joseph. He clapped Josh's steer on the shoulder and extended his hand to Josh, and the arena erupted with whistles and applause.

Josh Joseph had shown Practical County's Grand Champion Steer.

"You did a good job, Mule," I whispered as I stroked his head gently.

My head was down, and I didn't see the judge coming until his green boots were right beside Mule's front hooves.

The judge placed his hand firmly on Mule's neck and said, "Congratulations, young lady. You've got the Reserve Champion."

I shook his hand in disbelief as the applause pounded in my ears. Mule was Practical County's Reserve Grand Champion steer. It wasn't Grand, but it was Ryansmeade's highest award, and it was my very first try. I was so proud of Mule, and hoped Dad and Granddad would be just as proud of me. At the end of the arena, Dad was clapping and Granddad had two fingers in his mouth, and I heard his trademark whistle squeal out over the applause.

"We did it, Muley!" I shouted in his ear. "You and me, we did it!"

The judge took the microphone stand and started his explanation.

"This pair of animals before us here no doubt represent the best of Indiana's beef industry. I'll start with this handsome Shorthorn on my left. He's just a real nice . . ."

Josh and I pulled our steers to the center of the ring, where cameras flashed and the judge's voice continued, but I don't think I heard a word.

When the judge finished, a fresh-looking Lil Darling came prancing out into the arena, sash and tiara prominently displayed, proudly fulfilling one of her final duties as reigning Beef Princess. She looked as if she had completely recovered from the disgrace her sister had suffered just minutes earlier.

Lil's pink-and-white-striped skirt and jacket looked crisp and clean, but her four-inch white heels kept sinking deep into the manure and sawdust in the show ring. She seemed minimally disturbed by the manure as long as the cameras kept flashing while she presented Josh and me with our trophies and rosettes.

Soon the pictures were done, the crowd began to mill around, and I pulled Mule to the gate where the whole family waited.

"My grandchildren are so proud of you!" Frannie bounced around. Mom gave me a big hug.

"You were wonderful out there, Libby." Mom beamed.

"You bet she was!" Ronnie exclaimed. "And who taught you everything you know?"

"Um, Dad?" I teased.

Ronnie pretended to be hurt, and then grinned from ear to ear.

"I'd say *all* of Ryansmeade can collectively share in

tonight's success," Granddad said thoughtfully, "with the greatest share going to you and this fine fellow."

He squeezed my shoulder and gave Mule an affectionate pat.

Carol Ann leaned in close and whispered, "You got the Darlings in this competition, Lib! One down, one to go!"

"Here, let's hang your rosette on Mule's halter, and I'll take a picture of the two of you," Mom suggested.

I had to admit, Mule looked great with that big red ribbon streaming down the side of his face. His blue eyes blinked and he took in all the camera flashing and hugging with a calm that I knew even sweet Piggy couldn't have mustered.

"Didn't I say this fellow had potential?" Dad boasted.

"Yes, Dad, you did," I admitted. He had seen it in Mule from the very beginning. "I think I underestimated Mule."

"I believe I underestimated someone else," Dad said, his face serious and regretful. He put one arm firmly around my shoulders. "I underestimated my little girl, who has just proven in no uncertain terms that showing cattle can indeed be a girl thing."

It was a reward far greater than a ribbon of any color.

"I'll tell you something else, Libby girl." Granddad pulled one of my braids. "All of Practical County is talking tonight. They're saying, 'That Ryan girl is one fine showman.' Yes, sir, they'll be keeping their eyes on you and your animals for years to come."

I was happy like I'd never been happy before. It was like floating on a cloud. And I didn't think I'd ever come down.

Then I heard Mayor Thompson, who never missed an

opportunity where there was a crowd and loudspeaker to tell everyone what a fine town we had in Nowhere, Indiana.

"The Practical County Fair is the pride of Nowhere," he boasted from the podium, "and I want you all to come back Saturday evening for the Practical County Fair Livestock Auction. Folks, I'm telling you, with animals as fine as the ones you've seen here tonight, you're not going to want to miss this one. Bring your checkbooks, bring your neighbors, 'cause, folks, we're gonna sell some beef!"

Suddenly that cloud I had been floating on took a nose-dive, brought down by the mere thought of parting with Mule. *Clouds are just air, Libby,* I told myself. *And clouds can't stay up in the air forever.*

Eventually, what goes up must come down.

TWENTY-SIX

— the end of an era —

"I can't believe I'm doing this," I said.

"I can't believe you didn't do it before."

Carol Ann tied the long sash at the back of my dress as we stood before the full-length mirror in my bedroom. After months of thinking about the Beef Princess pageant, I could not believe it was here. I was far more nervous about this than I had been about entering the show ring for the first time. Maybe it was because Mule would not be by my side. There was no animal to hide behind. All eyes would be on me.

"Bow or knot?" she asked.

"Knot, of course."

She laughed. I looked in the mirror.

"You know I am totally against beauty pageants," I said matter-of-factly.

"This is *so* not a beauty pageant, Libby, and you know it! Think of it as a public service. Now sit."

Carol Ann was wound up. She spun me around and nearly pushed me into a chair, where she proceeded to touch up the makeup she had carefully applied to my face. "Don't add any more color," I warned her. "I don't want to look like a—"

"Darling?" Carol Ann finished.

"I was going to say clown."

Just then, Mom appeared in the doorway. She froze.

"What?" I asked.

"Look at you! You are absolutely gorgeous! Isn't she, Carol Ann?"

"Mom!" I protested.

"Yes, Mrs. Ryan, she looks awesome!"

Part of me wanted to get out of that silky blue dress and into some holey blue jeans. But some other part of me was pleasantly surprised by what I saw in the mirror. The Libby Ryan who looked back at me was a totally different person than the Libby Ryan whose reflection I usually saw. It wasn't all bad to look good.

Earlier in the week, Mom and I had managed to reach an agreement about hair. She wanted to take me to the salon for an elegant updo, complete with sparkly hairpins and a whole can of hair spray. I wanted my ponytail. We agreed on some hot rollers and a little bit of hair spray. The result was a soft curl just fancy enough to not be ordinary but still a long way from glamorous. I just didn't think I could do glamorous.

Dad came in.

"Are we ready to go?" he asked.

He, too, stopped in the door. What was with the doorway? Enough with the freezing in the doorway. It was like someone had covered it with plastic wrap so that everyone who tried to come through it bounced right off.

"Whoa! Back up the apple cart!" Dad did a double take.

"Dad!"

Carol Ann was cracking up.

Dad made his way through the invisible barrier.

"Is this the same girl who was sweating in the show ring earlier this week?"

"Charlie, we have a lot to do here." Mom ushered him out of the bedroom. "Why don't you go pull up the van?"

"Do you remember your beef breeds?" Carol Ann asked.

"Yes, I know them all."

"Remember not to walk too fast," Mom coached. "This is a pageant, not a race."

"I know, Mom."

"Oh, and be sure to spit out that gum. Judges hate chewing gum," Carol Ann advised.

Okay. That was enough coaching. It was time to get this over with.

The activities tent was packed despite the heat of the evening and the threat of thunderstorms. Parents with video cameras took front-row seats while grandmothers fanned themselves with the programs Lil Darling was handing out to all who entered the tent, perhaps her last official duty as Beef Princess.

I had my eyes peeled for Precious. Surely, since it was Ohma, and not me, who had turned her in, she wouldn't try to make good on her threat to sabotage my dress before the pageant. Especially now that it was *on* me. But then again, I wouldn't put anything past Precious.

The eleven contestants were pulled back behind the curtain to the staging area for instructions. Once we heard Mr. Fields, who was the master of ceremonies, start the show, we shuffled to our seats in our high-heeled shoes.

It wasn't until we were all seated that I realized that Lil was here without Ohma. Surely Ohma wouldn't miss the pageant.

I scanned the audience. I caught a glimpse of Frannie with two empty chairs beside her. I pitied the poor soul who attempted to sit on Eugene. There was no sign of Ohma, but Mr. and Mrs. Darling were sitting front and center with Precious right beside them. A strange, sympathetic feeling passed over me. Why hadn't Ohma decided to participate in the pageant? Was she still so devastated over losing her steer? What had her sisters done to her after she exposed Precious's dishonesty?

My thoughts were broken by the squeal of feedback from the microphone. Mr. Fields, looking flushed in his suit jacket, was center stage mopping the sweat from his forehead with a white handkerchief. The pageant was under way.

The first round of questions was easy enough. Tell us

your name, your grade in school, and why you like living in Practical County. Most of the contestants, like Karen Elliott and Jennifer Joseph, had done this before, making repeated attempts to beat the Darling duo.

Karen stepped out onstage, smiling, as if there weren't a hundred people packed into a hot tent and watching her. I prayed for half the poise she possessed.

When it was her turn, Lil strutted to the microphone and straightened her tiara as if to remind the judges that *she* was the incumbent. She had forgotten to spit out her ever-present bubble gum, which she popped and snapped into the microphone as she spoke. Out of the corner of my eye, I caught Carol Ann mouthing, "I told you so."

"Next," Mr. Fields announced.

I looked around. No one moved. The stage and tent were quiet. I realized everyone was looking at me.

How could I be so stupid? I jumped up from my folding chair too quickly and knocked it over. The metal chair hit the stage floor with a deafening crash. I tried to pick it up and stepped on the hem of my dress. There was a long, loud *rrrrrrrrrrrrip* and I looked down to see a ten-inch tear in the bottom of the dress, my heel still attached.

Obviously, I didn't need Precious to destroy my dress. I was doing a great job all on my own.

Bending down, I hopped on one foot to the microphone while I freed my shoe from the fabric. There was nervous laughter from the audience, and Mr. Fields tried to make me feel better by making light of my clumsiness.

"Well, Miss Ryan, take it easy now." He patted my shoulder. "Don't be in such a hurry to get to the microphone. Take a deep breath, dear. Good. Go ahead and answer the first question."

I did just as he said and inhaled deeply, then let it out slowly. That was better. Now, I needed to answer the first question. Wait. What *was* the first question?

"Whenever you're ready, Miss Ryan," Mr. Fields said through his ever-present smile.

I stared out at all the people fanning themselves in the hot tent.

"The first question," Mr. Fields prompted.

Oh, yes, introduce myself. Okay, that was easy enough.

"Hi, um, I am Libby Ryan. I, um, I live fourteen and a half miles from Nowhere on my farm. Well, it's not my farm. It's my dad's farm. Well, really, it's not my dad's farm totally. It's my mom's too. And my grandfather's. Yes, it was my grandfather's farm first and now it is my dad's. And my mom's."

I was pretty sure I had just babbled more words in public in the last twenty seconds than I had in my entire life.

"Thank you. Libby Ryan, folks," Mr. Fields said, giving me permission to return to my seat while the audience clapped politely.

I was grateful to Karen Elliott, who had set my chair back up for me so that all I had to do was slide into it and pretend that no one could see.

The other girls took their turns all too quickly and we began the second round, the interview. Questions were chosen at random by Mr. Fields, and we were expected to answer until the three-minute time limit was up.

Karen was asked how she would promote the consumption

of beef to the public given America's recent concerns about eating too much red meat. I would have panicked, but Karen was smooth and creative with her answer.

As for Lil, she tugged at her tiara when she approached the microphone and flashed a brilliant smile directly at the judges, completely ignoring Mr. Fields. When he repeated the question a second time, she suddenly realized he was talking to her and giggled.

"I'm sorry. Can you repeat the question?"

"I asked you if you could tell us the impact BSE has had on the beef industry in America and how you would combat the negative effects of BSE."

The brilliant smile disappeared in a flash.

"Ex-excuse me?" Lil stammered. "I'm sorry. What is BSE?"

Mr. Fields looked nervously at the first judge, who nodded permission for Mr. Fields to help Lil out of her situation.

"Bovine spongiform encephalopathy."

"I'm sorry," came Lil's reply. "I don't know what you are talking about."

Again, the judge gave approval for Mr. Fields to elaborate. I squirmed in my seat to see if I could get a look at Carol Ann's face, but a tent pole blocked my view. It appeared she was sitting next to Frannie and quite possibly on Eugene.

Why couldn't that have been my question? Mad cow! Mad cow disease! I wanted to scream.

"Mad cow disease." Mr. Fields had read my mind for the second time that evening.

"Oh! Oh, of course, mad cow disease!"

And in a flash Lil's blinding smile was back.

Unfortunately for Lil Darling, the smile wasn't enough to cover the fact that she knew absolutely nothing about mad cow disease. She rambled incoherently for two minutes using phrases that started with "if I am elected Beef Princess" and "therefore." Finally the timer sounded and put us all out of our misery.

"So, in conclusion," she said, beaming, "I believe somebody ought to do something about that BS, um, BS-whatever disease."

She finished with a final gum snap and then returned to her seat. She had no clue that she had botched her answer horribly.

After the next few contestants had answered their questions, it was my turn, and this time I was ready.

I stood slowly, and put one foot carefully in front of the other until I was facing Mr. Fields.

"As you know," he began, "more and more of the corn being raised by America's farmers is going to manufacturing rather than to feeding livestock. What are these new uses for corn, and what can farmers do to keep their feed costs at an acceptable level?"

I looked straight at Dad. Not two weeks earlier rising corn prices had been the topic of discussion at the dinner table.

"Well," I started. Everyone was looking at me. Oh, how I wished I had a steer up onstage beside me. I'd be a lot more comfortable with a lead rope in my hand. Instead, I fiddled nervously with the thin blue ribbon that was tied around my waist.

"It seems that, um, people are getting smart and finding

ways to turn corn into gasoline and cola, and I've even heard about corn being used to make plastic, and that's good for farmers, but I guess that means that there will be less corn to feed our steers."

The timer was ticking. The judges were staring up at me from their table at the foot of the stage. I scanned the audience, unsure what or whom I was looking for, but there she stood. At the back of the tent was Ohma, not at all dressed for a pageant in khaki shorts and sneakers, a cool lemon shake-up sweating in her hand. She gave me a huge, genuine smile, then a thumbs-up.

I cleared my throat.

"Well, so, on our farm, my farm, well, not my farm but my dad's farm . . ."

A soft wave of laughter rippled through the audience, and I realized I was rambling again.

Wrap it up, Libby, you're almost done.

"On my family's farm, we raise the corn we need to feed our livestock. But I think that it would be good for the beef industry if people researched other feed options for cattle. That way if there ever was a corn shortage, we would have other ways to feed our animals."

"Thank you, Libby." Mr. Fields nodded.

The audience clapped.

I knew my answer wasn't particularly brilliant. And it certainly wasn't spoken eloquently, but I hadn't puked yet, and considering how my stomach was turning flip-flops, that was something to be proud of.

When each contestant had answered her interview question, the judges retreated behind the curtain for a few minutes before handing the all-important envelope to Mr. Fields. Jennifer's face was a greenish gray, and Lil was bouncing in her seat.

"It's a beastly hot evening, folks." Mr. Fields wiped his brow once more and stuffed his handkerchief into his pocket. "Let's do what we came here to do and crown a Beef Princess!"

The audience cheered in agreement.

"Without further delay, ladies and gentlemen, your new Practical County Fair Beef Princess is . . ."

Not me, not me, not me, not me. I closed my eyes and prayed. Of course, I'd entered this competition fully intending to beat Lil Darling, but if Mr. Fields called my name, I just knew I'd need that garbage can.

". . . Miss Karen Elliott!"

An ear-piercing scream rang through the tent. It didn't come from the winner. It came from an outraged Lil Darling.

"What? There has to be some mistake!"

Mr. Fields ignored the outburst as Lil's hysterical wails nearly drowned out his words.

Karen gasped in disbelief and stood up. The audience roared with applause and everyone was on their feet.

Lil cried in her mother's arms until Mrs. Darling demanded a recount of the three judges' votes, which took all of three seconds. The Darling family's era of royal reign had ended. Precious held her sister's hand as they marched out of the tent.

I joined my family and Carol Ann. Each of them had hugs and kind words. When I got to Mom, she hugged me extra hard.

"I'm sorry, Mom."

"Sorry?" she repeated. "What on earth for? You did a great job up there tonight."

"But I didn't win."

"Libby, we are your family. Win or lose, we support you."

She touched one of my loose curls and said, "I know you did this for me. Thank you."

"It wasn't so bad. But would you be terribly disappointed if I didn't do it again?"

Mom laughed.

"I had a feeling you'd say that. I promise not to make you into a pageant princess if that's not your thing."

Just then Frannie strode by wearing Karen Elliott's newly earned tiara.

"She let me try it on, what do you think? It's so me, isn't it?" Frannie flitted across the stage, one hand on one hip, making supermodel turns and dramatic stops.

I looked at Mom and we both burst out laughing.

"Looks like you may get your pageant princess someday after all, Mom."

"Okay, Frannie," Mom said as she snatched the little girl from the stage. "Let's go give that back to Karen."

Ohma hung around at the back of the crowd for a while before making her way forward. She smiled and gave me a hug. I'd never known she had such a pretty smile. I guess I had never really seen her smile much before.

"You were great up there!" she exclaimed.

"Thanks."

Ohma seemed to be dealing better with the loss of her steer. In fact, she seemed different altogether. Maybe she was beginning to recover from years of being in the shadow of Precious and Lil. There was one thing I couldn't help asking.

"Why didn't you do it this year?"

"The pageant? Oh, I know everyone expected me to because of Lil and Precious, you know. But I'm really not like them."

"Well, I'm glad you came," I told her. "Do you think Lil will get over losing?"

Ohma shrugged.

"That's a question for someone who cares."

Carol Ann, Ohma, and I laughed. Frannie was back and, seeing the opportunity to impress a new audience, she pulled Ohma by the hand.

"Have you met my grandchildren?" I heard her ask Ohma as she led her toward two empty chairs.

After the pageant, Dad suggested we head over to the Cattlemen's Club concession stand for burgers.

"We'll need to stop somewhere else and pick up a salad for Libby, though," he said, looking around for a place to grab something other than pork, chicken, or beef. There was no disappointment in his voice; he sounded very matter-of-fact. It seemed he had finally realized that I might never eat meat again.

But I had come to my own realization.

"No, Dad, it's okay," I said. "I'd like to eat at the Cattlemen's tonight."

Dad, Granddad, Mom, and everyone else stopped walking.

"Libby, you don't have to—" Mom started, but I stopped her.

"Mom, really, it's okay," I explained. "I've been thinking about what we do at Ryansmeade, and about Mule and Piggy. And you know what? When I decided to become a vegetarian, I really hadn't thought it out completely."

Everyone was listening, but Granddad especially seemed to be waiting to hear what I had to say next.

"Beef is a part of my life," I continued. "It's a family tradition that I want to be a part of."

"You can be a part of our family tradition, dear, without giving up being a vegetarian," Mom reminded me.

"I know. But I love raising cattle, showing cattle, and I've decided that I can love my steers and still eat beef. Besides"—I grinned—"I don't think I could possibly leave this fair without consuming a single Cattlemen's burger."

I had decided that supporting the beef industry was a better way to honor Mule and Piggy than boycotting it.

"Well, then," said Dad, "that settles it. I'm buying a round of cheeseburgers for the entire house!"

I sat down with my family, unwrapped the one-third-pound cheeseburger, and inhaled deeply. Never had so much thought gone into eating a burger, and I savored this one more than any I'd eaten in my entire life.

We had finished eating and were cleaning up our trays when I felt Granddad's hand fold snugly around my arm, his dark blue eyes serious.

"You've been thinking." He smiled.

I nodded.

"You know I wouldn't care a bit if you never ate another bite of beef for the rest of your life."

"I know, Granddad."

"With or without a blue ribbon, a tiara, or a cheeseburger, you are Libby Ryan, Beef Princess of Ryansmeade!" His eyes shone with pride.

I laughed at his drama.

"I may have competition," I told him, nodding in Frannie's direction. She and Dad had been engaged in a serious conversation, which had just ended with Frannie making a very adamant declaration.

"I am too old enough to have my own bull!"

Wow. Dad would really have his hands full with that one.

"Now, you know," Granddad said, returning his attention to me, "you've done a lot of very mature things this week. But the hardest part is yet to come."

I knew exactly what he meant. The hardest part *was* yet to come.

TWENTY-SEVEN

— going, going . . . —

The arena glowed in the summer night. The stands filled quickly with a chattery buzz as spectators carrying elephant ears and lemon shake-ups took their seats. From inside the barn, I caught a glimpse of Carol Ann on the bleachers with her parents. Ronnie was out there too, with Frannie. And Mom and Granddad. Dad stood at the end of the arena.

I couldn't think about anything. I had to keep my mind clear. No, not clear, blank. *Block it all out,* I told myself. I didn't hear the rustle of the impatient animals around me. I didn't hear the distant screams of the terrified, thrilled passengers on the Super Loop. And I tried my best not to hear the auctioneer's voice from out in the ring as he began his seller's song.

Beside me, my steer huffed as if trying to pull my thoughts back into the barn, away from the state of blankness I tried desperately to maintain.

Don't look, whatever you do, don't look.

If I looked I might see those beautiful eyes, framed so perfectly by those long, wispy lashes. It was bad enough that I could feel him tugging slightly at the lead rope, his every movement pulling me closer to his living, breathing side.

I ran my hand along his back and patted his smooth, sleek shoulder without looking at him. I mumbled to him to be patient. Stupid old steer anyway. His impatience only proved his ignorance. He didn't even know enough about what was going on not to want to go out into the ring.

Of course, how could he know? After all, Dad and I had bathed him and groomed him just the same as we had done for every show this past week. And here he stood in a fancy halter, thinking he was headed out for competition one more time. How could a twelve-hundred-pound steer possibly comprehend what would happen next?

Merely thinking about it brought the burn of tears back into my eyes. Hadn't there been enough tears in the past few days? *Get it together, Lib. You're not going out there bawling like a baby.*

Suddenly the line moved forward. The hindquarters of the stocky Shorthorn steer in front of us took a step and so did we. One step closer to the inevitable.

Don't listen. Don't look. Don't think. Just go. Just go.

The tears were actually easier to hold back than the awful urge to stop moving. I wanted to freeze time at this very second so I could throw my arms around him and squeeze.

So I could bury my face in his warm, soft neck and smell the sweet mixture of straw and shampoo. So I could tell him I loved him and I was so proud of him.

So I could say "Goodbye" and "I'm sorry."

The Shorthorn took another step and suddenly we were out of the barn and into the glaring lights of the arena. The urge to freeze was climbing to a higher place inside me.

Just go. Just go.

The lights of the ring were bright compared to the dim bulbs in the barns. Cameras flashed, some held by folks from the local newspaper, some held by parents anxious to capture the moment for future scrapbooks.

It was a fast-paced sale. The fair board knew they had to get all the animals through before the buyers got tired and went home. The buyers were mostly local businessmen, looking for some good publicity for their companies. A few politicians were scattered here and there, hoping a bid would gain a few votes in the next election.

I could hear the auctioneer banter with the livestock committee chairman over the loudspeaker.

"How long's it been since you were a young exhibitor, Wayne?" the auctioneer asked.

"Oh, it's been a good forty-five years since I first entered that sale ring, Hank," the other man chuckled, taking the microphone. "I have to tell you, folks, that first year I showed a great big Hereford named Oscar," he reminisced. "Big as an ox, tame as a house kitty."

Cute. Could we please get this over with?

But the man named Wayne continued to remember Oscar.

"Let me say something to these young exhibitors here

tonight. Kids, I understand how you're feeling right now as you prepare to enter the sale ring."

I really didn't want to hear any more. But on he went.

"As long as I live, I'll never forget that lump in my stomach as Oscar and I lined up for the sale."

I knew what was coming next. He was going to say that time heals all wounds, we'll get over it, life goes on.

"Let me tell you, folks, as I stand before you tonight, that old lump is still there, right in the middle of my stomach, as I remember my first steer."

Oh, for crying out loud! I bit my lip a little harder as the man's voice cracked. The microphone squealed with high-pitched feedback as he handed it over to the auctioneer once again and stepped off the platform, wiping his eyes with the back of his hand.

From where I stood, I could see ladies reaching into their purses for tissues. I hoped someone sitting near Mom had a mop. She was a sucker for sad stories.

Without warning, Josh was in the ring. The auctioneer called for the first bid, and someone shouted out. Josh's job was to keep his animal moving in front of the bidders, which he did with his head down. Was it getting to him to sell his steer? Big Josh Joseph, who had done this many times before?

Earlier, in the barns, I had overheard Mr. Darling giving Lil instructions.

"Try to work up a few tears, Lil. It gets those buyers every time."

It made me furious, the thought of Lil trying to cry just

to get more money for her animal while I stood there fighting tears with every ounce of energy I could muster. In the sale ring, Josh was surviving. I could too.

The auctioneer, a stout man in suspenders and a huge cowboy hat, hollered over the microphone for the bids to keep coming.

"This is your Grand Champion, folks. Buy this big boy and you'll have bragging rights for the next year!"

The bids bounced back and forth between several potential buyers as Josh and his steer made continuous circles in front of the auctioneer's stand.

"Going once, going twice . . ."

There was a long pause and silence in the arena.

"Folks, I've *sold* the Grand Champion Steer of Practical County!"

Immediately, Josh exited the ring on the other end and one of the cattlemen opened the gate in front of Mule and me. Instinctively, Mule stepped forward. It was what I'd been trying to teach him to do for months. He wasn't going to make this any harder, and for that I was grateful.

The loudspeakers were pointed directly at the ring and the auctioneer's voice blared a singsongy tune.

"And looky here, folks, at the nice young gal with her Reserve Champion steer. Isn't he a beauty? Who'll start the bidding?"

The lights were hot and glaring. I kept a tight hold on Mule's halter and whispered in his ear as we made one circle around the center of the ring.

The ring man hollered and whooped each time a bid

came in from the stands, but I was not listening. I kept my eyes fixed on Mule's big blue eyes and kept his head up high.

All at once there was a burst of applause and the exit gate opened. I had been so focused I hadn't even heard the auctioneer cry, "Sold!"

Outside the ring a man from the Cattlemen's Club was sorting steers onto trucks.

"Take him over there," he said, pointing to a livestock trailer parked behind the barn.

"And don't forget your halter," he called over his shoulder as I led Mule away.

"What?" I asked.

Suddenly, Dad was there.

"Don't forget to take your halter, the man said."

I looked at Dad. This was it. My head ached with the pressure of every tear I had held back all day.

"Do you want me to do it?" Dad looked at me with understanding.

"No, I'll take him."

I led Mule to the back of the truck, where two men waited to take him up the ramp. I removed his red show halter and stroked his clean, sleek black side one last time. I put both arms around his neck. He was so warm and soft and alive.

Mule's blue eyes blinked at me, and he took a step forward. He had no reason to linger there. He had no goodbyes to say. He simply wanted to move forward, just as I'd taught him to do.

I let go of him, and he was gone. I watched him disappear into the dark emptiness.

"Goodbye, Mule," I choked.

I turned from the truck and into Dad's open arms.

Afterward, Dad and I wandered through the arena, Dad chatting with folks he knew while I searched the crowd for the one person I knew would understand my loss. Mayor Thompson approached Dad and, after they'd exchanged a few words, Dad motioned me over.

I really didn't feel like talking, but I forced a smile as the mayor shook my hand and congratulated me on my Reserve Champion steer and sale.

"I'm proud of you, young lady," he boomed as he shook and shook and shook my hand until I thought my arm had turned to Jell-O.

Apparently, he wasn't the only one who wanted to congratulate me. Mom finally caught up with me (for once without Frannie attached to her leg), ready to gush.

She wrapped both arms around me and held on for a long moment. "You did so great tonight, Lib! I've never been so proud!"

"Thanks," I sighed. Everyone kept acting as if this night were something to celebrate. But I didn't feel like celebrating. I felt like leaving. Because everything at the fair reminded me of Mule.

"I know you really wanted to bring Piggy to the fair, but just look how well Mule did. Next year"—she grinned—"maybe it will be Grand Champion for the Ryan family!"

"I don't know," I answered. I had a head full of doubt that I would ever do this all over again. "Maybe I'm not cut out to show steers."

Mom looked surprised.

"Really? You're kidding. Libby, you should have seen yourself out there. You are a natural showman!"

"I am?"

"You bet you are. You've got animal smarts that most kids your age don't even know about. And in the ring, you and Mule were such a good team."

"But, Mom, I don't know if my heart will ever get over losing him," I choked out. The tears that I thought had dried up were back.

Mom nodded knowingly.

"Oh, Libby, that feeling you have tonight is one I understand all too well. I showed my first steer when I was thirteen."

"You did?" Why hadn't I ever heard this before?

"I didn't want to tell you, kiddo. Because after I found out how hard it was to let go that first year, I gave up. I never showed again, and I've always regretted it."

I certainly understood how she could give up. The pain of saying goodbye was so real and so awful, I really didn't want to do it again.

"But you know what?" Mom went on. "You have the potential to love and care for a lot of steers in the coming years. If you give up, some pretty sweet animals will miss out on your care and attention. Besides, they've also taught you a valuable lesson. They helped you learn how to say goodbye."

Fresh tears spilled out as Mom said, "Come here, kiddo."

I laid my head on her shoulder as we walked back toward the barn for the last time. The atmosphere across the entire fairgrounds was one of an ending. The amusement company had begun the task of tearing down and pulling out before dark. The concessions shut down, and a steady stream of livestock trailers poured out the gate. The Practical County Fair was over until next year.

TWENTY-EIGHT

— the future of ryansmeade —

Mom's words echoed in my head in the weeks that followed, when I'd walk into the big hip-roof barn and feel its emptiness. At first I was sure it was missing Mule that tugged at my heartstrings, but when the summer days started to cool and autumn leaves began to glide gracefully to the ground, I felt the emptiness turn to yearning.

If I closed my eyes, I could hear the rustle of cattle as they lumbered to their feet for their morning grain. I smelled the unique aroma of straw, grain, and manure. I saw the excitement of the show ring, the impressed look on the judge's face when he stood before my steer, and Dad's approving nod. But when I opened my eyes, I saw nothing, only bare pens and empty feed bunks. Perhaps it was time to fill that lonely barn with a fresh, new experience.

"You think this nice weather will hold through harvest?"

"Hope so."

Dad and Granddad both leaned their arms over the top rail of the white fence and gazed out over Granddad's pasture. The breezy, warm early-autumn evening would be one of the last before the frost came and the farmers began their harvest. Already the cornfields had turned from green to brown, ears pointing to the ground, a sure sign that picking time was just around the corner.

Mom, Frannie, and I surveyed the prospects. I wished Ronnie hadn't gone back to Purdue already. He would have had an opinion regarding the next star steer to come out of Ryansmeade. Granddad had quite a few calves, and some of them were pretty sleek.

As usual, the friendly ones were right there, licking and sucking our fingers. One skinny young Hereford tipped his curly red head back and stretched his neck when I lifted my arm in the air to avoid being devoured. His eager pink nose reached out time and time again. Persistent, that was what he was.

Several others skittered around the lot, charged by the evening air, the presence of new people, and the promise that feeding time was not far away.

On the far side of the lot, away from the others, there stood a lone Angus calf that caught my eye. He was just as young as the others, yet his sturdy frame was already beginning to show muscle. Indifferent to the rest of the herd or to the audience Frannie provided, he turned briefly in my direction and stared hard at me for one long moment. Then he slowly turned away.

Wow, he's got an attitude, I thought.

But animals with attitudes could change. So could people with attitudes, for that matter. I had learned that over the past year. It seemed that a negative attitude was sometimes the result of negative experiences. Ohma Darling was proof positive that a little kindness could go a long way.

Our last year at Nowhere Middle School had started. Carol Ann and I ate lunch with Ohma every day. Frannie had started kindergarten and hadn't mentioned her grandchildren in more than two weeks. Maybe she'd decided she didn't need them anymore. But to be honest, I kind of missed Eugene and Esmerelda Emily. I kind of wished I had tolerated them a little more when they were around, for Frannie's sake.

I guess that was what Mom, Dad, and Granddad did for all of us Ryan kids. They supported our dreams and decisions, no matter how big or odd they seemed. They helped me set up a savings account, and my check from selling Mule was the first to go in it. Funny, all along I thought Mule's purpose was to be the best steak he could be. But he did something even more meaningful—he made the first contribution to my education fund.

"Are you ready to get your new calves, Libby?" Dad asked.

I nodded.

"Why don't *you* tell *me* which two you'd like this time?"

Granddad said as evening turned the cornfields of Practical County a circus-peanut shade of orange.

I scratched the head of the little red-haired calf that hadn't left my side or let go of my fingers since we'd arrived.

"I like this little fella right here," I told him.

"Good choice," Mom agreed.

"Whoopie!" cheered Frannie.

Dad surveyed the rest of the herd.

"You've got one more. Which one's it going to be, Libby?"

I didn't hesitate.

"I'll take that Angus way over there."

Maybe he wasn't the friendliest one of the bunch. But thanks to Granddad and Dad, I'd developed a good eye for quality, and that little steer showed a whole lot of potential.

Granddad nodded in approval. "Looks like a winner to me."

"That's that," said Dad. "Let's load them up."

When we got the two little guys into the trailer and closed the gate behind them, they jumped around and bellowed, not at all certain they wanted to leave their pasture home.

"What are you going to name these sweet little fellows?" Mom asked me as we all piled into the pickup truck.

"Oh, Mom!" I declared with a wink in Dad's direction. "Don't you know that fair calves don't need names?"

Dad returned the wink, and two new calves were on their way to our barn, on their way to unknown adventures, and, maybe, on their way to the Practical County Fair.

The barn didn't seem nearly as lonely once we'd

unloaded the calves. They looked safe and comfortable in their new home. They looked like they belonged there.

"There you have it," said Granddad proudly. "There is the future of Ryansmeade."

Everyone nodded as they gazed at the new calves. But Granddad wasn't looking at the calves. He was looking at me, Libby Ryan, the next generation of the Ryan family farm.

MICHELLE HOUTS began her writing career with a retelling of "Jack and the Beanstalk." It earned her three metallic stars and a great deal of praise from her first-grade teacher. With no sequel in the works, she finished school, earning bachelor's and master's degrees in education. While at The Ohio State University, she met the farmer of her dreams. They married and made their home on a grain and livestock farm in west central Ohio, where they are raising their three children, along with cattle, hogs, a golden retriever, and a goat who believes he is a golden retriever. Ms. Houts is an elementary school special-education teacher and an adjunct faculty member at Wright State University, Lake Campus. *The Beef Princess of Practical County* is her first novel.